Gwen Lepkowski

Cross-Country Treasure Hunt

(And the Mystery That Followed)

By Gwen Lepkowski

Cross-Country Treasure Hunt
(And the Mystery That Followed)
by Gwen Lepkowski

Printed in the United States of America

ISBN 978-1-60647-638-3

"Home on the Range" by Dr. Brewster M. Higley and Daniel E. Kelley, early 1870's

www.xulonpress.com

Acknowledgments

With Thanks

To my dad, my mom, my sister, Beth, and my brothers, Royce, Dan, and Sam, who went on a cross-country adventure with me. This story would not exist without you.

To my husband, Paul, and my boys, Michael and Luke, for helping to make this dream a reality.

To Mrs. Beth Long and her third grade class: Alex, David, Eben, Harrison, Jessica, Joshua, Kenny, Michael, Nathan, Natalie, and Paul for their input and enthusiasm.

To Dan and Zack for their help with pictures and to Madison and Megan for the sacrifice of their time.

To God for creating such wondrous things and for treasuring us.

> "…you will be my treasured possession." (Exodus 19:5 NIV)

> "We love because He first loved us" (1 John 4:19 NIV) and "laid down his life for us" (1 John 3:16 NIV).

Record their journey on a map!

As you read this story, you may choose to color in each state that Josh Reed and his family enter. Then you can see where they have been and where they might go next on this treasure hunt adventure.

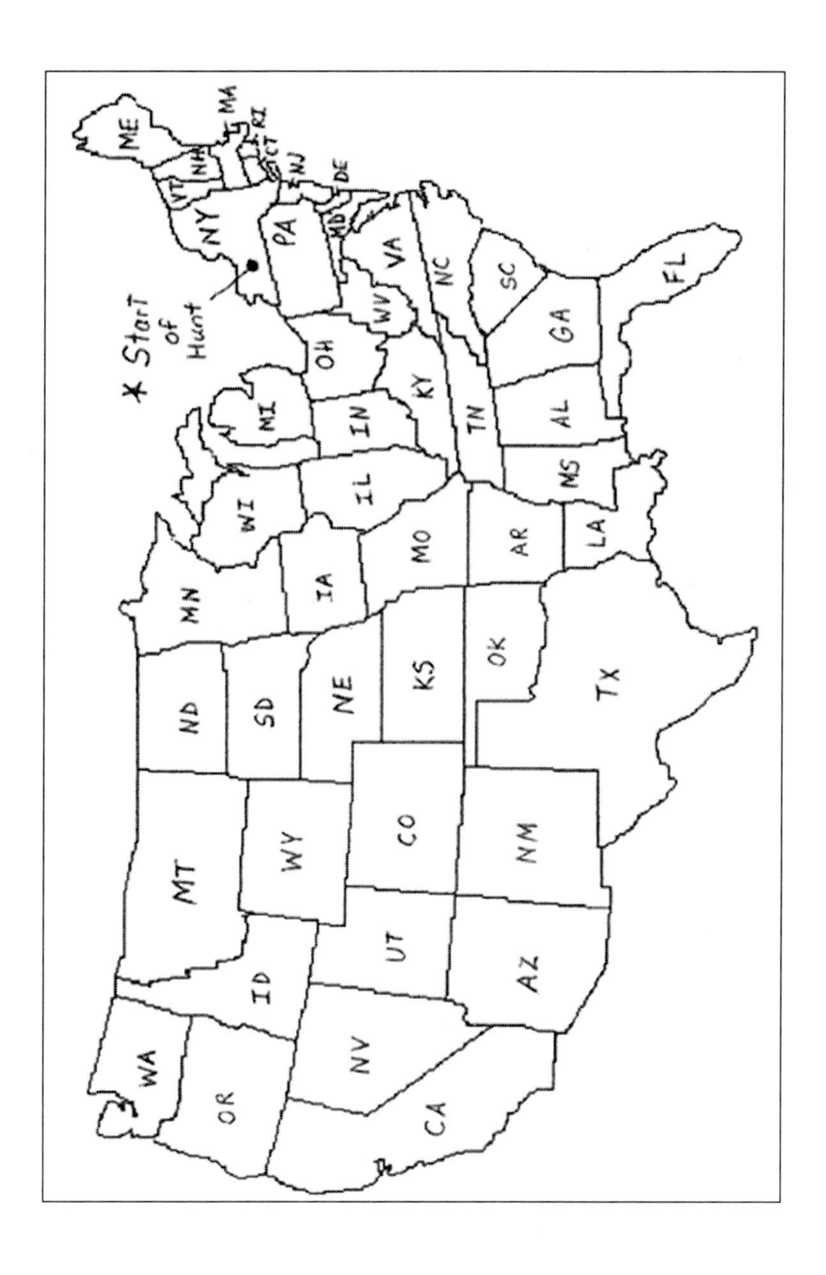

* Start of Hunt
ME
NH
VT
MA
RI
CT
NJ
DE
MD
NY
PA
VA
WV
NC
SC
GA
FL
OH
MI
IN
KY
TN
AL
MS
IL
WI
MN
IA
MO
AR
LA
ND
SD
NE
KS
OK
TX
MT
WY
CO
NM
ID
UT
AZ
WA
OR
NV
CA

Contents

Chapter 1 The Treasure Hunt 11
Chapter 2 Ready or Not, Here We Come 17
Chapter 3 Following the First Clue 23
Chapter 4 Strange Noises 31
Chapter 5 Lost! 37
Chapter 6 Tornado 45
Chapter 7 Another Storm 53
Chapter 8 The Bat Cave 61
Chapter 9 Sand Dunes 67
Chapter 10 Rockhounds and Canyons 73
Chapter 11 In the Zone-Arizona 79
Chapter 12 Airplane Adventure 85
Chapter 13 Lava Tubes 91
Chapter 14 Four Corners 97
Chapter 15 Petrified 103
Chapter 16 Death Valley 109
Chapter 17 Giants 117
Chapter 18 Bears or Sharks? 123
Chapter 19 Yellow Stones and Yellowstone 131
Chapter 20 The Chase 139
Chapter 21 The Treasure 145

Chapter 1

The Treasure Hunt

Hiding behind a spruce tree, he waited. He shifted his weight from one foot to the other as he looked down the long driveway with woods on either side. Twenty minutes had already passed.

The boy with thick brown hair and green eyes decided to climb the prickly evergreen. It was a hard, uncomfortable seat, but at least he was sitting now. His green clothes blended into the tree as he had planned. Very quietly, he watched and waited. It should be soon, very soon.

"Hey, Josh!" eleven-year-old Brittany called, greeting her twin brother from below.

"Ah!" yelled Josh as he almost fell out of the tree. Fortunately, he had good reflexes.

His twin sister grinned. "What are you doing? Being a spy again?"

"You'll see," Josh assured her.

Just then Josh heard a chickadee call. It sounded like a short high whistle followed by a short low whistle. Josh returned the call his older brother had made. Fourteen-year-old Will poked his head out of an upstairs window and yelled, "Anything yet?"

Josh shook his head. Then he heard the rumble of a car. "Brittany, hide!" he whispered urgently.

Her blue eyes wide, Brittany still was not sure what her brothers were involved in this time, but she played along and slipped behind a tree.

The car was coming closer. Would Will's latest invention work? Josh wondered.

If it worked, the car would pass in front of the motion detector alarm that he had helped Will make. When it sensed the car passing in front of it, they would hear...

Suddenly, loud music blared from the motion detector and the device in Will's hand. "It worked!" he called above the racket.

As Will hurried outside to show Josh, everyone came running to see what was going on. Mom and Ella came from the kitchen. Brittany popped out from behind the tree. Six-year-old Isaac jumped down from the swing set. Josh climbed down the tree.

"Please, Will," Mom implored, "turn that thing off!"

"Sorry, Mom," Will said sheepishly as he flipped a switch. "You see, the motion detector tells us that..." Will looked at the person coming toward them. "Dad's home."

Dan Reed walked calmly toward the group gathered on the driveway. "It was the strangest thing. I was driving up the driveway when I thought I heard music blaring."

That was all it took to launch Will into an explanation of the new security system he had made himself. "The music turns on and lets us know someone is there. Plus the loud music can scare intruders away," he finished.

"Impressive," Dad had to agree, "but a little loud. I don't think we want to hear that every time we come up the driveway."

"I'll work on it, Dad." Will grinned as he started thinking again.

Josh wondered what the alarm would sound like the next time. Knowing Will, he would probably make it say something hilarious. If there was anything Will liked as much as a good invention, it was a good joke.

Dad held the mail in his hands. As he flipped through it, he noticed one large envelope in particular. "It looks like something from Nana. Since everyone is here, should we open it?"

A chorus of excited chatter answered his question. The family tromped into the living room and sprawled on the furniture and floor. Josh sat on the sofa but leaned forward in anticipation.

Nana was not a typical grandma, and her letters always told of her latest adventures.

"Ooh, I wonder where she is now," Brittany said as she looked at Nana's pictures displayed on the wall. "Russia? England? Mexico?"

"I wonder what she is *doing*," Josh emphasized.

Isaac jumped up and down. "Maybe she rode in a submarine again."

"Or went horseback riding," Brittany wondered.

"Or flying over the Grand Canyon," Ella added.

"Or skydiving with a shark." Will grinned.

"Will," everyone groaned.

"Well, you never know," Will said.

Mom decided to end the speculation. "Let's find out, shall we? Dan, are you ready to read? Dan?"

Dad had been skimming through the letter and now had a strange look on his face. He ran his hand over his beard. "You are never going to believe this."

"What? What?" everyone wanted to know.

Dad started to read:

My dear family, Dan, Linda, Ella, Will, Brittany, Josh, and Isaac,

What a glorious time I am having as I travel the country. From deserts to snow-capped mountains, from ocean to ocean, it is amazing to see all that our Lord has created.

Then I thought of you. Do you remember, Dan and Linda, when you talked of taking the children out West on a trip across the country to see the wonders of God's creation? It must be time. Your dear Ella is already seventeen and will be leaving for college in the fall. This is the summer that you must take that trip.

Now for the fun part. I have decided to help you along in this little adventure. I have made a treasure hunt for you! With this letter you will find sealed numbered envelopes with clues inside. If you follow the clues, they will lead you across the country to many wonderful places. At the end I will be waiting with a treasure for you. In case you are wondering, I am not at home. I will be staying with some friends, so you will just have to use the clues to find me. What fun!

I sincerely hope you will take me up on this offer. You know I like "real" letters better, but since I am not at home, e-mail me if you are coming on the treasure hunt.

I love you all.

Love,
Nana

At first there was stunned silence and then a clamor of voices. "Can we, Dad? Mom? I think we should go." As a student in a homeschooling family, Josh had an idea that might convince his parents. "It could be a field trip. The best ever!"

Mom and Dad looked at each other. "We have been wanting to take the kids out West," Dad said.

"It's true that Ella will be leaving for college in the fall," Mom acknowledged. "Maybe this is the time for us to go."

It was settled. Josh went to his bedroom and returned with his detective journal. As the others discussed trip ideas, Josh opened his journal and looked at the important questions listed inside. Who? What? Where? Why? When? How? He began to write.

Who? (That was easy.) His family

What? A trip

Where? From home (upstate New York) across the country

Why? A treasure hunt

When?

How?

Hmm. Those still needed to be answered. "Mom? Dad?" Josh asked. "When are we going? How are we going to get there?"

"Good questions," Dad said. "It is already June so the sooner, the better."

"But how?" Mom asked. "All we have is our old van." She thought for a moment. "How about a pop-up camper that the van could pull behind it?"

The Reed family e-mailed Nana. They were coming.

Chapter 2

Ready or Not, Here We Come

Two weeks later, they were ready. Josh sat back against the seat of the van and remembered all the preparations they had made. A secondhand pop-up camper was purchased. Mom and his sisters sewed curtains to hang in its windows and cleaned it thoroughly. Josh, Will, and Isaac helped their dad remake the roof of the camper with new supports. Then they painted it. Dad spent many hours working on the van while Mom bought and packed canned and dried food for the trip. The kids helped wash and pack summer clothes. They also packed anything else they wanted to bring on the trip. Josh brought adventure novels and his detective journal.

Now Will sat next to Josh and glanced at his detective journal. "What's that for?" he asked.

"Well, I want to write the answers to Nana's clues to find her and the treasure. Plus, you never know when a mystery might happen," Josh said.

Will looked thoughtful. "Yeah, you never know."

Dad and Mom closed their van doors. Everyone was here. "Are we ready?" Dad asked.

Six enthusiastic responses answered his question. An air of anticipation could be felt as Dad pulled out the first envelope

and opened it. Josh wrote "First Clue" in his detective journal and then closed his eyes to concentrate as Dad read the first clue.

> Head south one state and look around;
> A famous groundhog is what you've found,

And a place to camp just miles away
In Paradise, you're welcome to stay.

Josh opened his eyes. "South one state is Pennsylvania," he said, "but isn't Paradise another word for heaven?"

"Yes, and I sure would like to go there," Dad joked, "but I think Nana has something else in mind."

Will leaned forward. "Well, I know who the famous groundhog is. Punxsutawney Phil is the groundhog they watch on Groundhog's Day to see if he sees his shadow, so we must be going to Punxsutawney."

"I think you're right," Dad remarked, "and Nana owns some land just a few miles north of there in Paradise Settlement where we can stop for the night."

"Is there really a place called 'Paradise'?" Brittany asked.

"More than one actually," Dad chuckled.

"Maybe they named it that because it is so beautiful there," Brittany said.

"Let's go see!" Josh enthused. Next to "First Clue," he wrote "Pennsylvania."

"Punxsutawney, here we come!"

Brittany turned to her twin. "This is so exciting. I can't wait to set up camp tonight in Pennsylvania. The pop-up camper is so cute. It will be so much fun!"

They had been traveling about half an hour when Mom and Dad started looking at the temperature gauge on the van with concern and had a quiet conversation. Josh could tell something was wrong.

"Kids, I am so sorry," Dad began, "but it looks like we will have to turn around. Our van is struggling. I thought it would be able to pull the pop-up camper, but with us and our things to carry too, it just won't work. The trip would be too long and any mountains would be too steep for our old van to handle."

"We can't give up," Josh said with a note of desperation in his voice.

"We'll see what we can do," Mom said, "but for now we have to go home."

Life isn't fair, Josh thought. Then he had a better thought and prayed quietly: "Lord, we feel pretty sad right now. Could You please show us a way to go on this trip? Thanks. In Jesus' name. Amen."

It was a quiet half-hour home.

The next day Dad brought home a small inexpensive flatbed trailer. It looked like a wood floor on wheels. Josh, Will, and Isaac helped Dad build plywood walls and a lid on it. Now it was a box on wheels! The box would hold the family's tent, sleeping bags, small mattresses, pillows, a tarp, food, clothes, a lantern, and a Coleman stove. This would be much lighter for the van to pull.

At first Mom and the girls were not happy about camping in a tent every night, but slowly the family's good humor was returning.

Josh, who practiced watching people so he would be a good detective or spy someday, noticed that Brittany still looked down. He walked over to his twin and tried to cheer her up. "Remember? This will be fun."

"I don't know, Josh. This is not how it was supposed to be." Brittany sighed. "I mean, I wanted to sleep in a bed, not on the ground."

"But now it will be even more of an adventure. Think of the stories we will have to tell."

"I'd rather not, Josh." She smiled weakly. "But thanks for trying to cheer me up. I'll try to look forward to this trip anyway."

Ella waved and called to the twins, "Come on over and help us name this box trailer. When pioneers went West, they went in prairie schooners, so I thought we should call it Prairie Schooner, but Will here thinks we should name it Tumbleweed or Tornado."

"What's wrong with that?" Will grinned. "It might be appropriate."

Brittany looked thoughtful. "How about Explorer?"

"That sounds just about right," Ella said as she hugged her sister.

The next day was the Fourth of July. The seven Reeds, with Nana's clues in hand, were back in their van and ready to go. "Lord, please watch over us," Dad briefly prayed with his family, none of them knowing the dangers they would soon face along the way.

That is how it came to be that the Reeds camped across America. This time there would be no turning back. The adventure had begun.

Chapter 3

Following the First Clue

"What time is it?" Josh asked from a back seat.

"2:15," Mom answered.

Josh entered the time in his detective journal beside "Start of Hunt."

The Christian radio station played patriotic music for the holiday as they traveled.

Ella started singing along, then Brittany joined in, and soon everyone was singing along to a familiar song. *The beginning of an adventure must put people in a good mood*, Josh thought.

At 4:20 p.m., they saw the sign that told them they were entering Pennsylvania. Everyone cheered.

"We have entered my old stomping grounds," Dad called from the front.

Josh looked out the window and saw oil wells, oil pumps, and a factory making products from crude oil.

A sign said, "Borough of Louis Run."

"Where we live, we might say it 'Town of Louis Creek' since a run is another way to say creek," Dad commented.

"This is bear country," Dad called back again. The Allegheny National Forest crowded in on both sides of the road, and a thunderstorm lit the sky in such a dazzling display of lights that the kids felt it was better than any old fireworks display. Josh eagerly looked out the window for bears as they drove through rain and between foggy forested mountains.

"There! Stop!" Josh cried, pointing. A large animal lumbered out of the forest into an area with many old fallen trees and heavy green growth.

The van slowed down and stopped as the Reed family watched the bear. In return, the bear turned and curiously watched the van before heading back into the dense forest.

"That was amazing!" Josh exclaimed. Everyone agreed. Josh wrote in his journal, "July 4th - bear sighting."

"Dad," Isaac asked, "why did the trees fall down here?"

Now that the bear had left, the family gave the forest itself a closer look. *A mystery,* thought Josh. *Oh, good!*

"Well, it looks like these trees fell down a few years ago. See how the fallen trees look old and plenty of high green vegetation has grown up in place of the thick trees that used to shade the ground?"

Sometimes it helped that Dad was a science teacher, Josh thought.

"Does anyone see any other clues to the mystery of the fallen trees?" Dad asked.

"I don't think the trees were chopped down by a person because they look broken off," said Brittany. "And the trees are broken higher off the ground, instead of down lower."

"Good observation, Brittany. Anything else?" Dad drove farther to see more of the broken trees.

"It's like a path," said Will. "The broken trees started over there, crossed the road, and go that way. But the other trees around look fine."

"That's right," Dad acknowledged.

Josh thought hard. What could break trees as if they were toothpicks and leave a path of destruction like that?

"A tornado!" Josh cried.

"Where?" Brittany's wide blue eyes looked fearfully at the sky.

"No, I mean, did a tornado do this, Dad?" Josh asked.

"Good work, Josh," Dad said. "My guess is that a tornado came through here a couple of years ago."

Josh wrote "tornado damage" in his detective journal.

"I'm hungry, Mom," Isaac called.

"It *is* dinnertime," Mom said. "Dan, let's take a driving break."

"That sounds good," Dad said.

"Ella, could you please reach the sandwiches?" Mom asked.

"Sure, Mom." Ella handed out the sandwiches, and they all ate in the van.

"Does anyone need to stretch their legs?" Dad asked.

"Dan, what about the bear?" Mom reminded him.

Dad touched her hand, reassuring her. "It's probably long gone, and we'll stay close to the van."

Dad and the boys hopped out first. Josh looked around and wondered if a bear would emerge out of the mist. Things seemed quiet.

Then Josh noticed a nearby bush. Red raspberries! Yum. "Dad, look," Josh said, gesturing to the bush.

Dad confirmed that the berries were indeed raspberries. "Dessert!" he called to Mom and the girls in the van. Soon everyone was picking and eating raspberries.

I bet the bear would love these, thought Josh, but the bear did not return.

Instead, the Reed family climbed back into the van and continued deeper into Pennsylvania.

Josh looked out the window and saw a sign that said Johnsonburg. As they passed by piles of wood chips, Isaac said, "Eeww, what's that smell?"

"A paper mill," Dad replied.

On they drove through Reynoldsville and some other little places until finally they were there. "Punxsutawney!" Will shouted.

They eagerly looked out the windows for any sign of Phil the groundhog. "I see him!" Isaac cried. "Well, it's a statue of him."

"There's another groundhog statue!" Josh reported. "It's taller than me!"

"And that groundhog statue is wearing clothes," Will remarked with a grin.

The Reeds parked the van and decided to walk around. They found out that Punxsutawney Phil had a wife and children too when they visited the Groundhog Zoo. After visiting the groundhogs, the family walked around a little more before heading back to the van. Brittany swatted at a tiny fly biting her arm. "These little flies are so annoying."

Will was thrilled to be able to tell her. "Guess what I read? Punxsutawney actually means 'Town of the Ponkies' which is what the Native Americans called the little sand flies. Town of the Little Flies! Isn't that great? I guess Punxsutawney has been known for something besides just groundhogs."

"I'm ready to go to Paradise," Brittany remarked.

The Reeds returned to their van. Soon they drove through Paradise Settlement, and it *was* beautiful with wildflowers and lush green grass and forests. Dad showed them some churches and the old one-room Pifer schoolhouse. "Does that name sound familiar?" asked Dad.

Ella knew. "Pifer was Nana's maiden name. Can you imagine having a school building with your name on it?"

Josh grinned. "Of course, since we have school in our house, that's sort of like having a Reed schoolhouse."

The sun was setting. With darkness swiftly approaching, the Reeds finally reached Nana's land. It was a little after 9:00 p.m., and they needed to hurry. Setting up the tent could be a little tricky without light. Everyone gratefully pulled themselves out of the van. After Dad unlocked and opened the box trailer, everyone helped unload the tent, sleeping bags, mattresses, and pillows.

Josh dumped the tent frame pieces on the ground and grinned. It looked like a puzzle with poles of different shapes and sizes.

They had to get this thing together. The kids began grabbing pieces. "Here, Isaac," Ella said, holding out her hand. "See the green dot on your piece? It connects to this piece with the matching green dot." Brittany helped slide the tent material onto the poles. Josh found more pieces to connect. When all the pieces were in place, there was a large frame for the middle, a medium frame for the front, and a smaller frame for the back of the tent. Dad helped them get the tent standing and showed them how to pound the stakes into the ground to keep the tent from falling over. Will and Josh finished pounding stakes just in time before darkness fell.

With flashlights and giggles, the Reed kids passed mattresses, sleeping bags, and pillows into the large two-room tent while Mom arranged where everyone would sleep.

"I don't want to sleep near the side, Mom. Put me in the middle please," Brittany requested.

"Why don't you want to sleep near the side?" Josh asked.

"I figure it's safer. That way any bears will step on or eat you first," Brittany teased.

Josh laughed and threw a pillow at his twin.

Will decided to join the fun. "We *are* in a corner of a field near the edge of the woods. I bet this is a great bear area, prime bear territory."

Brittany wrinkled her nose at him.

"How about a snack before bed?" Mom offered after the tent was settled. Mom pulled out bags of popcorn.

"That looks good," Will said as he took a bag and began to munch.

"Be careful not to drop it on the ground," Ella reminded them. "We don't want any furry company tonight."

"Company can be nice," Will teased. "We could leave a trail and see what comes to visit."

Finally, after cleaning up and brushing teeth, Josh took off his shoes and entered the tent. The mattresses were soft under his feet. He found his pillow and sank down onto his sleeping bag with his navy blue flashlight close beside him. This would be the ultimate camping trip, he decided happily. Who else gets to camp all the way across the country?

"Ow!" Josh yelled and moved his leg out of the way.

"Sorry, Josh. I didn't mean to step on you," Brittany said. "I was just trying to walk to my sleeping bag."

"That's okay. Isn't this cool?"

"The mattresses are a nice touch," Brittany decided. "I'll tell you what I think in the morning."

Suddenly, Brittany gasped. "Josh, what's that?"

Josh sat up and heard growling. He saw a huge shadow looming on the wall of the tent. It came closer and closer.

Something hit the tent wall. "Rarr! Did I scare you?" Will's voice asked.

"Not me," Josh answered.

"Come on, Will." Mom's patience was coming to an end. "It's time for bed."

"Okay, Mom," Will answered.

Soon everyone was in bed and settled for the night.

Just as Josh was drifting off to sleep, he thought he saw a bright flash outside the tent. Maybe it was a distant thunderstorm, he decided. He watched for more flashes but none came. *Maybe it was just my tired eyes playing tricks on me*, Josh thought as he drifted off to sleep.

At 7:00 a.m. Josh awoke to the sound of a rooster crowing. Listening again, he realized it was not actually a rooster but his dad crowing along with a distant rooster. Josh groaned at the wake-up call.

Then Josh remembered and sat up suddenly. "Get up, everybody. We get to read Nana's second clue today!"

As everyone ate some cereal and sticky buns, Dad opened the sealed envelope which contained their second clue and began to read:

> They say it never ends.
> Go southwest to Hoosier friends.
> It is time to go spelunking.
> Dan, do you remember something?

"That has a lot of words that I don't know, Dad," Isaac said.

"Hmm. Hoosiers are people who live in Indiana," Dad said.

"So we are going to Indiana." Isaac smiled.

"What's spelunking?" Josh asked.

"It means exploring caves," Dad explained.

"Cool! We get to explore caves? Nana is the best!" Josh gave Will a high five.

"But where in Indiana, Dan?" Mom asked. "The clue indicates that you would know."

Dad leaned back and rested his hands in the grass where he was sitting. "I think I can figure this out," he said thoughtfully. "When I was a boy, we lived in Indiana for a while. The clue says, 'They say it never ends.'" Dad thought for a moment. "I've got it! My mom and dad used to take me spelunking in a certain cave. No one knew where the cave ended. I remember hearing that after forty-nine hours of exploring the people still had not reached the end so they had to turn around and come back. I don't know if that's true or not, but that must be the place."

"Indiana, here we come!" Josh cheered, his eyes sparkling with excitement.

Chapter 4

Strange Noises

"He did *what?*" Josh exclaimed as they passed through Big Run.

"Practical jokes." His dad chuckled. "Great-Grandpa Edison used to work in that old brick hardware store and play practical jokes on his friends who came to buy things."

Maybe Will inherited his sense of humor from him, Josh thought.

After telling some family history, Dad was suddenly all science teacher. He pulled the van over to the side of the road and hopped out.

"What are you doing, Dad?" Josh asked out the van's open door.

"I want to add to my rock collection," Dad called back.

Josh rolled down his window and felt a breeze lift his sweaty hair off his forehead. That felt better.

Dad was bent over, picking up some black rocks, but he still managed to carry on a conversation. "This is coal from Pennsylvania. I hope to get a rock from every state we travel through. Would you like to join me?"

"That's a great souvenir idea, Dad," Will decided. "It's like taking a piece of the state home with you."

Mom found some plastic bags, and soon everyone had a piece of coal in their own labeled bags.

The wind was picking up more, Josh noticed, and the sky was darkening. A few raindrops pelted the dry ground. As lightning streaked across the sky, the Reeds dashed to the van and made it inside just as the thunder shook the car. "Does that mean we are 'as quick as a flash'?" Will joked.

The others laughed, partly with relief.

Dad started driving but did not go far before the heavy rain made it difficult to see. He pulled over to wait as the rain pounded on the roof and lightning danced across the sky.

"I don't like this," Isaac said and hugged Ella, who was sitting next to him.

Ella hugged him back. "It will be over soon," she encouraged.

Josh noticed the rain slackening. As the rain lessened, Josh could see a black car behind them that had also pulled over to the side of the road. Was it following them? *No,* Josh told himself, *it must be waiting for the storm to pass too.*

The storm did pass and the Reeds entered Ohio. Dad said they were leaving the Appalachian Mountains behind. Josh noticed that the land was getting flatter. Still, the little hills, trees, and farms reminded Josh of home even though they were now in the Midwest.

Mom's travel book showed a camping area nearby, so that night the Reeds set up camp in a state park. This time the Reed kids were a little faster at setting up the tent, and they did it without help! Ella went to watch Isaac on the playground while Mom and Brittany went to get some pizza for everyone.

As Josh was looking around this new campsite, he heard a *thud* in the woods. "Dad, is that you?" Josh called.

"I'm in the tent, Josh," Dad answered.

"I thought I heard something in the woods," Josh explained.

"It was probably a small animal like a squirrel or chipmunk," Dad called back.

"Okay, Dad," he said, but Josh was not so sure.

He heard the noise again. *Thump!* That did not sound like a squirrel.

"Will, where are you?" Josh called.

"Right here." Will suddenly appeared behind his brother.

Josh jumped. "I thought maybe you were in the woods," Josh explained.

"Not me," Will said.

Josh felt braver with Will there. He started walking into the woods with Will close behind.

Thunk!

"Did you hear that?" Josh turned to his brother.

Will was stretching and yawning. "Hear what?"

"That noise," Josh insisted.

Will listened. "I don't hear anything. It was probably a bird or someone spying on us." Will's green eyes sparkled with mischief. "Of course, you are the detective in the family. If anyone is out there, let me know."

Josh knew Will was just joking, but what if there really was someone out there?

Maybe he would have to be even more observant from now on. If there was something going on, he would find out.

The next day, July 6, could only be described by one word: hot! A radio station forecasted central Ohio to reach 90 - 95 degrees. The Reeds were heading south now through rolling farmlands.

At 2:07 p.m. Josh wrote in his detective journal: "Entered Indiana at last!" Still, it would be hours before they reached their destination.

Dad was concerned that the van might overheat while carrying them and pulling the box trailer Explorer in the heat, so he did not want to use the air conditioner too. That meant Josh and the others had to roll down the windows to stay cool. It was a loud ride as air rushed around them. Ella, who had been reading to them on the trip, could only read two chapters aloud before her voice wore out. It was just too loud.

Mom and the girls had covered their hair with colorful scarves to keep their hair from blowing in their faces and ending up in hopeless knots.

At least the refilled ice chest has cold drinks, Josh thought as he sipped some cold soda. Outside the window, he could see the land becoming flatter. They were near Indianapolis now.

"Rock stop!" Dad called through the rushing air. The van stopped in a hilly wooded area. Since Dad had lived in Indiana before, he knew this was a good area to hunt for geodes. "Just look for round lumpy rocks," Dad called as he headed for a creek bed. The kids found what Dad had described.

"Hey, Dad," Will said, "there are other rocks around. Can we find something a little more interesting? These look so generic. They're boring."

Dad just smiled and handed Will a hammer. "Crack it open, son."

Will just stood there uncertainly. "What did you say, Dad?"

"Give it a whack."

"Okay, Dad." The others stood back to give him some room and watched.

Will hit the rock, and suddenly they saw beautiful crystals of purple and white that had been hidden before.

"Wow, Dad." Josh was amazed.

"Can I try it?" Brittany asked. When Brittany cracked her rock, pink crystals sparkled at her. "It is so beautiful," she breathed.

When it was Josh's turn, his geode broke in half to reveal orange crystals. "How do they get in there?" he wanted to know.

"Water can get into rocks with holes in them and deposit various minerals inside that form crystals over a long period of time," Dad said, "but geodes can show us even more."

Dad continued. "If you see a geode on the outside, it looks so dull and ordinary, but inside it is spectacular. Geodes always remind me of people. Do you remember the

Bible verse, 'Man looks at the outward appearance, but the Lord looks at the heart'? Sometimes people only see the outside, which may seem ordinary, but God sees who we are inside. When we give our lives to God and let Him work in our hearts, He can make something spectacular. Of course, it also reminds me not to decide what someone is like by just seeing what they look like, but to get to know them and see who they really are inside. Does that make sense?"

The others nodded. Josh knew he would never forget the message of the geodes.

While walking back to the van, Josh noticed the plants he passed were not the same kind as those at home, and the bugs walking on him looked different too. Mom, who had studied plant life in college, said the trees with grapevine-shaped leaves and white-grayish bark were sycamore trees. It was hot too, but they were almost to the cave.

Chapter 5

Lost!

"We're here!" Dad announced. "I think." The temperature had reached 100 degrees during the day, but now it felt cooler at 96 degrees. They had traveled until evening, but the Reeds finally reached the cave valley. The gate was open so they drove through but then stopped abruptly as the road disappeared down a steep incline.

"Does the road really go down there?" Mom asked.

"I don't know. It looks different since I was here last," Dad admitted.

Josh wondered: if they drove over the edge, would the van flip over or get stuck? They left the van and walked down the steep road to see what lay beyond.

Eventually they found the new owners. Apparently, the camp had been closed, but now they were fixing things up and preparing to open it to visitors again. They told the Reeds they could stay there for twenty-five dollars.

The family returned to the van and looked again at the steep road. Carefully, they drove the van over and down the incline while Mom gripped the seat and Isaac exclaimed, "This is fun!"

The van did not flip over. Breathing a sigh of relief, the Reeds looked for a camping spot. "Let's camp beside that little stream," Mom suggested.

The family started to unpack the box trailer when Josh had an idea. "Let's time ourselves and see how fast we can set up the tent."

"I've got a watch," Ella volunteered.

"Let's do it," Will agreed.

"Ready, set, go!" Ella cried.

The Reed kids quickly assembled pieces, raised the tent, and pounded stakes. Then they threw in the mattresses, pillows, and sleeping bags and arranged them on the floor of the tent.

"Done!" Josh yelled.

"Twelve minutes," Ella announced. "That's not bad. Maybe next time we'll be even faster.

"Now we can get to the caves," Josh said.

"Oh yeah," Will agreed.

"Wait a minute," Mom said as she stirred the soup heating on the Coleman stove. "It's time to eat, and it's dark. I don't want you getting lost in a cave." She started pouring soup into bowls.

Dad looked longingly toward the caves. "You know, Linda, I could go with them. Just for a quick look."

Mom gave Dad her "I'm serious" look.

"We would take flashlights and just stay in the cave openings," Dad assured her.

Mom reluctantly agreed, so after dinner, Dad with a lantern and Will and Josh with flashlights in hand started out through the night to find a cave. At least it was a clear night and the moon gave some light.

"Cave ahead," Will whispered.

"Why are you whispering?" Josh asked.

"It just seems like the thing to do at night."

The cave was on the side of a hill and had a stream flowing out of it. Dad went first, stepping carefully onto one moss-covered rock and then another. The lantern light reflected off the cave walls. Will went next. "This is great!" he said, his voice making a hollow echo sound. "I wonder if there are any bats in here," he added as he shone his flashlight at the ceiling.

"They are probably all outside," Josh reminded him, "since they go out at night and sleep during the day."

Josh had just taken one step onto a slippery rock in the cave entrance when he saw it. A short flash of light came from the woods near the cave. "Who's there?" Josh called.

"What's wrong, Josh?" Dad turned around to look at him.

"I saw a flash of light outside."

"Are you sure it wasn't light from our lantern bouncing around?" Dad asked.

"I'm sure," Josh said. "It was outside." He scanned the woods with his flashlight.

"Maybe it was a firefly," Will offered.

"No, it wasn't," Josh insisted.

The three guys left the cave and looked around but saw no sign of anyone.

"It's getting late," Dad said. "Let's head back and we'll explore more tomorrow.

As they entered the campsite, Mom was really glad to see them safe and sound.

Everyone else settled into sleep, but Josh tossed restlessly. He was beginning to wonder. He had seen two unexplained flashes of light on this trip, heard strange noises in the woods, and seen a suspicious black car. Could these things be related? Could someone be following them? If so, why?

By the light of his flashlight, Josh opened his detective journal and began to write on a fresh page:

Mystery?

What happened:	Where:
Flash of light	Pennsylvania
Black car following them?	Pennsylvania
Noises in woods	Ohio
Flash of light	Indiana

Josh yawned. Maybe these things had simple explanations, but just in case there was a case to solve here, he would be ready. He closed his journal and drifted off to sleep.

The next morning Josh felt better. Why had he let his imagination run away with him? He breathed in the refreshing air. This forested little valley with the cold stream flowing out of the cave felt warm, but it was like a cool oasis compared to the heat they had endured yesterday.

As they were eating breakfast, Isaac spotted something interesting. “Look, it’s a stick that’s walking!” he cried.

The others crowded in to see.

“Close,” Dad said. “It is called a walking stick, but it is really an insect.” The walking stick was six inches long with beautiful red and green markings.

Later that morning, the family went to explore the cave.

“Oh, this is cold!” Brittany said in surprise as she stepped into the water in the cave. In places, the water was up to their knees, so they rolled up their pant legs and kept going.

“Look, a salamander!” Josh said and pointed at the creature hiding in the rocks.

As they walked, they saw rocks with different patterns and textures.

Suddenly, a huge crayfish crossed their path. Brittany tried to get out of the water onto a rock ledge. “I’m ready to go back,” she declared.

“It’s okay, Brittany,” Josh said. “All it can do is pinch you.”

"I know. That's why I'm ready to go. Who knows what else is in here," she added.

That sounded great to Josh. He would love to see what else was in there.

Mom, Ella, and Isaac were ready to go too so Dad led everyone out of the cave with a lantern. Then everyone went back to camp except for Dad, Will, and Josh, who wanted to explore more caves.

After two more caves, Dad and Will were ready to return, but Josh wanted to look in just one more cave.

"Okay, Josh," Dad said, "but I'm waiting here." He tied a line of rope onto Josh. "Just make sure you don't take this line off. When you are done exploring the cave, you can follow this line back out again."

"Okay, Dad," Josh said. Then he left Will and Dad behind and entered the dark cave with just his flashlight.

He had gone a long way when he heard a noise. It sounded like flapping ahead, and he could see a tiny bit of light.

Unfortunately, he had come to the end of the line tied around him. He could not go another step, but he really wanted to see what was ahead. If only he could go just ten more feet... Josh remembered what his dad had said about leaving the rope on, but maybe he could slip it off–just for a minute. Then he would put it back on again. He wouldn't go far.

Josh untied the rope and walked toward the noise. He shone his light at the ceiling.

A bat suddenly flapped its wings only inches from his face.

The movement startled Josh. His flashlight clattered to the ground. The light went out. How would he find his way back now? He wouldn't be able to find the rope in the dark cave.

He couldn't see the rope, but farther ahead he could see a little glimmer of light.

Josh kept walking farther and farther toward the light. Maybe there was a way out.

Then he found the light's source. Looking up, he saw daylight streaming through an opening in the ceiling of the cave. He looked at the slippery rock walls and the opening fourteen feet above him. This was no way out.

Josh sank to the floor and put his head in his hands. Why, oh, why had he taken off that rope? How would he get out now?

A brief moment of panic tried to take hold, but he pushed it aside. He had to stay calm. He had to think.

Maybe someone would hear him if he called. Josh stood up again and cupped his hands to his mouth. "Help!" he yelled. "Help!" The sound of his voice bounced around in the cave, but no one answered.

He knew someone who could hear him, though. "Help, God. I've really done it this time. I'm sorry. Please help me out of this mess."

His dad and Will knew where he was, Josh remembered. Maybe the Lord could stir their hearts to come look for him. He sat down to wait.

Meanwhile, Will looked at Dad. "Josh has been in there a long time," he said.

"We have been here a while," Dad agreed. "Let's get Josh. Just give the line a tug to signal him."

Will pulled. "Hey, Dad. I don't feel Josh on the other end."

"Don't pull anymore," Dad instructed. "Let me try." Dad stood up and pulled, but the rope did not become taut. Dad's face became concerned. "He's not attached.

Will, you stay here. If I'm not back in twenty minutes, I want you to go back to camp and tell your mom what is happening." Then Dad grabbed the lantern and quickly entered the cave.

"Josh!" he called. "Josh!" There was no answer. Dad followed the slack rope until it ended. "Josh!" he called.

"I'm here, Dad!" came Josh's voice. Then Josh was running toward the light of the lantern and into his father's embrace.

"Thank You, God. You're safe," his dad said with relief.

Josh told him what had happened. "I am so sorry."

"I know you are, Josh. Let's get back to camp."

Nineteen minutes after his dad had entered the cave, Will saw a welcome sight. With a whoop of relief, Will ran to his dad and brother who were emerging from the cave.

The Reeds had done enough spelunking for now. It was time to move on. Back at camp, they read Nana's third clue:

> Where pirates used to hide and wait,
> along the Ohio River banks.
> VACE-NI-CORK

Mom got out a map. "The Ohio River is too long for us to follow it, looking for where pirates used to hide," she told them. "We need to know where it is exactly."

"Maybe VACE-NI-CORK is a code," Josh offered.

Brittany jumped up excitedly. "I've got this one. The words are scrambled. See? Switch the V and C and it says CAVE. Switch the N and I to spell IN. Switch the C and R to spell CAVE-IN-ROCK."

"Is there such a place?" Josh asked.

"Got it," Mom said, pointing to a spot on the map. "Right here in Illinois. Good work, Brittany."

Josh had a great thought. "Do you want to be my partner someday when I have my own detective agency?"

Brittany smiled. "We'll see."

"I guess we're not done with caves yet. Cave-in-Rock, here we come," Will cheered.

Josh wrote the clue and answer in his detective journal. *Next clue, here we come,* he thought.

Chapter 6

Tornado

Crossing a bridge over the Ohio River, the Reed family drove into Kentucky and stopped at a state park for the night. The trees provided some welcome shade against the intense heat, but the little black flies and mosquitoes were not so welcome.

"Help, I'm being eaten alive!" Will called as he ran past Josh. "I really am. I'm alive and I'm being eaten."

Josh shook his head and headed for the showers. He was just thankful this park was nice and clean and had running water. Boy, did he want a cool shower. It was 10:00 at night and the day had cooled to 90 degrees.

The shower felt good, but as soon as he stepped out, beads of sweat began to form on his forehead and roll down his face again.

The next day, the Reeds crossed the Ohio River again, but this time they went by ferry. As they drove their van onto the barge, the kids were bouncing with excitement. They had never been ferried across a river with their van before.

"Look at the tugboats," Ella said excitedly.

"That tugboat is pushing six barges," Brittany noticed.

Isaac started counting. "One, two, three, four, five, six, seven, eight. That tugboat must be really strong to push that many barges!"

Soon the Reeds were being pushed across the river too. As they drove off the barge, they saw that they had crossed from Kentucky into Illinois.

Mom decided to wash clothes in an air-conditioned laundromat while the others visited a souvenir shop and went to a park with a playground. As Josh looked around the park, he suddenly had the strange feeling that someone was watching them. Turning, he saw a man in sunglasses slowly driving a black car by the park. Maybe he should tell his dad, Josh thought, but the car sped up and disappeared around the corner. It was probably nothing, he decided.

After a picnic at the park, the Reeds were ready to visit Cave-in-Rock. This was a dry cave with a wide opening overlooking the Ohio River. "Outlaws, river pirates, and bandits used to hide along the riverbanks and attack unsuspecting boats to steal their riches," Dad explained. Josh thought this did look like a good place to hide.

"I wonder if they left any gold hidden in here," Will wanted to know.

"I doubt it," Dad said. "This cave is visited by many people. Someone would have found something by now."

"I think I'll still look," said Will, heading to the back of the cave.

A minute later, Will returned. "Hey, Josh, come see what I found."

Josh followed Will to the back of the cave. Suddenly a pirate voice said, "Arr, Arr, Arr. Are you looking for me gold?"

Josh looked startled and Will began to laugh. Will picked up his mini-tape player on which he had recorded the pirate message.

Josh thought it was pretty funny. Then he began to wonder. What if Will was the one making noises and flashes of light to give Josh a mystery to solve? He would have to watch Will more carefully.

"This looks like a good place to read Nana's next clue," Dad called. "Anyone interested?"

The Reeds huddled around the next clue as Dad opened envelope number four and began to read:

It is not so "bad," "Carls."
Stalactites, stalagmites,
Beauty underground
But what about all of these
Bats flying around?

Silence. Then Josh said, "This is a tough one, but bats live in caves, so is it another cave?"

"Can I please see the note, Dad?" Ella asked.

Dad handed the note to Ella. "Stalactites and stalagmites are definitely in a cave," she told Josh, "but which cave?" She read the first line again. "It is not so 'bad,' 'Carls.'"

"Why did Nana write 'Carls'?" Isaac wanted to know. "None of us are named Carl."

"That is strange," Ella agreed, "but see how she put 'Carls' and 'bad' in quotation marks so we would notice them?" She showed Isaac the note.

Then she thought. "Carls bad. I got it! Put it together!" Her eyes lit up. "There is a cave called Carlsbad Caverns. There are a lot of bats there too."

Josh hoped if he saw another bat, he wouldn't drop his flashlight this time.

Mom got out her map and announced, "It looks like we are heading to New Mexico."

"That is a long drive," Dad said, "but we can make some stops along the way."

The Reeds entered Kentucky again and found sandstone as their state souvenir at a cut in the rocks.

When the Reeds crossed the Ohio River for the third time, Josh began to wonder if they were really going anywhere. They passed through a small part of Illinois and then crossed the Missouri River right before it joined with the Ohio River to become the Mississippi River.

They had entered Missouri. Dad, always the teacher, called back to the kids, "The Mississippi River bottomland is flat and has rich soil from flooding." As they drove, Josh could see irrigation systems. One was watering corn. They drove by fields that were flooded with ditches. Brittany turned to Josh. "I wonder what they grow there? Rice?"

Josh shrugged. "Maybe." He was relaxing against the seat now that the day was cooler thanks to some clouds blocking the hot sun. He looked up at the sky. A wall cloud rose up beside them as they drove.

"Those wall clouds can turn into tornadoes," Dad said. "So keep your eyes open. We are in tornado alley."

Josh watched. Missouri was the "show-me state," or so a sign said. Maybe it would show them a tornado. It would be so great to see a tornado, Josh thought. Then again, they did not have a basement to run to if one did come their way. He would like to see a tornado but not get swept up in one. Josh watched for a while but did not see any tornadoes, at least not yet. His eyes felt heavy and he drifted off to sleep.

When he woke up, they were still in Missouri, but not near the river anymore. Then he saw it, a thin funnel-shape in the distance. "D-D-Dad!" he stuttered. "Look!" He pointed out the window.

"Well, what do you know," Dad said. "A tornado!"

Brittany and Will were now leaning over Josh and had their faces pressed to the window. "Let's get out of here!" Brittany wailed.

"Dan, we do need to find shelter," Mom said nervously.

"We will," Dad said. He started going faster. "See if you can tell which way the tornado is moving."

"It looks closer, Dad," Will stated.

Josh remembered reading about tornadoes. They would have to leave the van. His family could lie in a ditch and cover their heads if they had to, but it would be better to have shelter. The tornado did look closer, and the wind was now blowing strongly.

"Dad, what about that house?" Josh asked.

Dad zoomed into the driveway, ran to the door, and knocked loudly. No one answered. He knocked again and called out, "Hello! Please, we need shelter! A tornado is coming!"

"Over here!" someone yelled. A door in the ground opened and a head poked out. Dad rushed back to the van to get the others. "Come on!" Josh and his family rushed to the root cellar through the rain and wind. The trapdoor opened to let them in and then shut. They were under the ground.

By the light of a lantern, the Reeds could see their hosts. Dad shook hands with a man with thin graying hair and then with his kind-looking wife. "Thanks for helping some strangers," he said.

"No problem," the man replied. "We have to help each other out. Besides, the Bible says that sometimes when we take in strangers, we are entertaining angels. Are you angels?" the man asked with a twinkle in his eyes.

Dad smiled. "No, I'm Dan Reed and this is my wife, Linda, and our kids: Ellen, Will, Josh, Brittany, and Isaac."

"I'm George Marlow and this is Doris. I'm just glad our root cellar is extra large to fit all of you."

"You sound like Christian people too," Dad said. "Would you mind if we pray about that storm over our heads?" The new friends prayed for safety and huddled and talked while the tornado prowled above them.

Finally, it was quiet. Josh was thankful that he and his family were safe, but he did wonder if their van would still be there or if it had been swept up by the tornado.

The Reeds and Marlows came out of the root cellar and looked around at the wind damage. "Thank You, God!" Mrs. Marlow cried in relief and hugged her husband. The tornado had not touched their house. The Reeds were relieved too. Their van was still there.

The Marlows asked the Reeds to stay for a dinner of fried chicken and spend the night too. Josh liked camping, but sleeping in a real bed felt wonderful.

The next morning the Reeds left after hugs and exchanging addresses. They felt like close friends because of what they had been through together.

In the Ozark Hills of Missouri, Dad called, "Rock stop!"

"That's a whole lot better than the tornado stop we made yesterday," Will joked.

They all piled out. Dad said that the rocks they were collecting were called chert. As Brittany went to pick up a rock, she gasped. A lizard was running through the rocks. "Look!" she cried.

"Wow, it's the first lizard we've seen out here!" Josh said excitedly. "Did you see how fast it is?"

That night they camped in Willow Springs, Missouri. The next morning the family left at 9:27 a.m. or 10:27 a.m. They could not decide which. It started when Mom turned her clock back one hour and announced, "It is 9:27 a.m. Central Standard Time." They were in a different time zone. Ella turned her watch back one hour too.

Dad began to joke around. "Well, now, maybe I should just stay on Eastern Standard Time so I don't have to keep adjusting to new times as I travel."

"But, Dad," Brittany said, "what if we need to know when something starts? We need to be using the same time as everyone else in the area." This time Josh sided with Brittany.

"Not me," Will joked. "I'm going on Pacific Time, so if we go that far west, I'll be ready."

The Reeds ended up leaving the van's clock time on Eastern Standard Time (the time at their home) and set their watches for Central Standard Time (where they were now).

In southeastern Missouri, the Reeds decided to stop at Laura Ingalls Wilder's historic home. Isaac wondered why they were stopping when Laura was not there to visit, but Mom explained that they could walk through the museum.

As they pulled in, a black car pulled in behind them. Josh saw a man wearing sunglasses inside. Josh had an idea. This time he would get the license plate number. Then if he saw a black car again, he would know if it really was the same car. As the others chattered and walked into the museum, Josh quietly carried his detective journal and pen. He quickly scribbled down the license plate number in his journal as they walked past the car. It was a New York license plate. Had it followed them from their home in New York?

Inside the museum, Josh drew a shaky breath as he tried to learn about Laura and Almanzo Wilder and their hard pioneer life, but it was the Bible verses that Laura herself had written down to use in times of her life that really helped him settle down. She liked Hebrews 11 to remind herself about what trusting in God can accomplish and John 14 for peace.

Back in the car again, Josh looked behind him and saw only shocks of wheat. No black car was following them.

Chapter 7

Another Storm

The Reeds crossed into Kansas and Dad made another rock stop. This time the Reeds found flint. Josh looked around at the grassy flatland and recognized black-eyed susans growing beside the road, just like home. Dad said they were in the Great Plains. It was 103 degrees that day. *This is too hot*, Josh thought.

That evening as they drove into Oklahoma, Isaac spotted something out the window. "Look, look!" he cried. "What are those?"

"Buffalo! Cool!" Will said.

Dad pulled over and everyone hopped out to see the buffalo ranch. Most of the buffalo were farther away, but one was right at the fence. Josh got his camera and took a picture. Besides the buffalo, a long-horned cow, chickens, a rooster, ducks, and peacocks wandered around. They also saw a beefalo, which Josh had never heard of before. It was part cow and part buffalo.

"How about burgers and fries for dinner?" Dad offered.

"Okay!" the others agreed until Dad bought the burgers under a sign that said "buffalo burgers."

"Dad, I can't eat a buffalo," Brittany pleaded.

"Why not?" Dad asked. "You eat cow burgers."

"I know," said Brittany, "but at least we call them hamburgers so we don't have to think about eating cows."

The Reed kids looked warily at their buffalo burgers. "I'll go first," Dad said as he took a big bite and chewed it thoughtfully.

"Is it good?" Mom asked.

Dad took another bite. "It is quite good. It tastes a lot like hamburger."

Mom took a bite. "It's good," she told the kids.

The Reed kids started eating their buffalo burgers. Josh thought it tasted a lot like hamburger, but not quite. Even Brittany finished her burger but said she still liked hamburger better.

"But now you can say that you have eaten buffalo," Josh said. "Another experience on our adventure."

That night the family camped in Heyburn State Park near a lake with white egrets landing in the water and flying above it. They set up the tent in the shade of small waxy-looking oak trees. The soil in which they pounded the tent stakes was reddish-brown, and the green grass actually had a few cactuses mixed in.

Working together, the Reed kids set a new personal record. They set up the tent and filled it with mattresses, sleeping bags, and pillows in seven minutes. "All right!" Josh exclaimed.

When Josh lay down to sleep on his sleeping bag that night, the noisy insects, seventeen-year-old locusts, kept him awake. That is when he saw it again—a flash of light!

"Will, Will, wake up," Josh whispered. "I saw it again."

"Huh, what, saw what?" Will struggled to wake up.

"A flash of light," Josh explained.

"Maybe it was lightning." Will yawned and turned over.

"No, Will. Please, let's go look."

Will got up, although he was still groggy. The two boys grabbed their flashlights and unzipped the tent. Outside the tent, they shone their flashlights around but saw nothing. The boys went back inside the tent.

Will thought it was nothing, but Josh felt almost sure now that something strange was happening.

The next day was beautiful. It looked as if someone had torn up cotton into small pieces and scattered it across the wide blue sky. As they drove, Josh saw oil wells that looked like giant grasshoppers and oil tanks too.

Dad saw something also. "It's an armadillo!" he exclaimed as he pulled the van over to the side of the road. Everyone looked out the windows, trying to see. Dad hopped out and walked into the deserted road. Ella held Isaac's hand as everyone exited the van. Then they saw it.

"Ew! Road kill!" Brittany said and turned away.

"But we don't have road kill like this in New York," Will said as he stared at the dead armadillo.

"At least we get to see one up close this way," Josh said.

Brittany took a quick look and headed back to the van.

It was not long before they passed through Texola, a border town between Texas and Oklahoma. Josh liked how they put two words together to make a new word. Maybe he could think of two words to combine to make a new word too. How about putting chicken and potatoes together? They could be chickatoes.

While they stopped for gas, a wind picked up the dust and whirled it around them.

Here in Texas, Josh saw a cotton field, some wild sunflowers, and soft grayish-green sagebrush at a picnic area. Texas had a lot of oil wells and cattle too, Josh noticed.

When Will saw a windmill that pumped up water for the cattle to drink, he joked, "I wonder if when those cattle get thirsty, they start blowing on the windmill to get water." That brought some laughter despite the 102-degree heat.

Then Josh had a joke and asked, "Where do you find the Great Plains?" No one figured out his joke, so he told them, "In great airports!"

Farther into Texas, the Reeds decided to stop and take pictures. Isaac found a large multicolored grasshopper and a tarantula hole. Ella was being careful to avoid some thorny grass with tips like arrows that work their way into the skin, but she stepped on some grass stubble that went through her cloth sneaker and into her foot. She had to return to the car. Dad decided to look for rattlesnakes in a ravine.

Josh looked through the lens of his camera at the grass, brush, and ravines or gullies. Oh, no! A big gust of wind blew the hat off his head and sent it soaring across the prairie. Josh chased it. When he finally caught it, he saw something else. Was that a black car waiting in the distance?

Josh walked way back to the van to get his binoculars and then set out again to get a good look at that car. He was close enough now. He stopped and focused the binoculars. If he could just see the license plate, he would know.

Way back by the van, Dad was calling, "Everyone in the van! A storm is coming!"

Josh had been so intent on finding out about the car that he had not noticed the ominous dark rainclouds that were swiftly approaching. The Reeds were taking shelter in the van. "Come on, Josh!" Will shouted. Josh could barely hear him.

Josh began to run toward the van, but it was so far away. That is when it began to rain in diagonal sheets so hard that Josh could barely see. He stopped. Where was the van?

A streak of lightning hit the ground, and almost immediately thunder crashed. *That was close,* Josh thought. He suddenly realized that he would make a good lightning rod standing there. He hit the ground and lay flat. Around him the lightning flashed and the thunder boomed.

Josh's mom was really worried. "We have to do something," she cried. "Dan, can you see him?"

"It's raining too hard," Dad answered. "I'll go after him."

"But you don't know where he is," Mom cried.

"I have an idea," Dad said. He honked the horn.

Josh heard the honk and began crawling toward the sound. He heard more honking. Josh stood up but hunched over to stay as low as possible as he ran toward the sound. He was closer now. He could see the van through the rain.

Then he was there pounding on the door. Will quickly opened it and pulled him inside. "Thank You, God!" Mom cried. "Honey, are you all right?"

"I'm okay," Josh said, grinning. "Just really, really wet."

The prairie thunderstorm did stop eventually, but it was evening and they needed to find a place to camp for the night. The only place around seemed to be Palo Duro Canyon State Park, which took them back toward the storm again. The land looked flat, but was there really a canyon nearby as the name implied? If there was a canyon, would it be wise to stay there during a storm? Would it flood?

The Reeds prayed and decided to head to the state park. Thankfully, the storm was only on the edge of the camping area. After paying an entrance fee, they followed the edge of "Texas' Grand Canyon" and then circled down into the canyon's depths.

"Should we be concerned, Dan?" Mom asked as they drove by an upright marked stick in the ground that looked as if it measured how high the water could rise there. It looked like it measured the water in feet.

"We will be okay," Dad said. "There is no water right now and the storm is passing." Five times they crossed areas marked by sticks. Everyone was feeling a little nervous, but they decided to set up camp. It was not their fastest setup time. The tent stakes did not stay well in the red, sandy soil, but eventually the tent was up.

That night Josh's sleep was interrupted by flashes of light and loud booms, but these were not mysterious sounds. He knew exactly what they were. The loud thunderstorm woke everyone and sent them scrambling to the van where they waited out the storm. Thankfully, no floodwaters rushed in.

More storms came, but the Reeds decided to stick it out in the tent since the storms were not directly over them. Brittany climbed back into her sleeping bag. "The tent must have leaked. My feet are wet!"

"Be glad it's just your feet," Josh said. His sleeping bag had been directly under a leaky seam.

"There's room here," Isaac said.

Josh moved over. "Thanks."

"Just try to find a somewhat dry place to sleep," Mom said, "and we'll dry things out in the morning."

Flashes continued to light up the tent, and the thunder crashed. The wind threatened to blow the tent over, and rain dripped through the seams. Eventually the night calmed and the family slept.

Josh awoke the next morning to the sound of his older sister's voice. "Oh, it's so cute! Come see. I've got to get my camera."

Brittany scrambled to the tent opening just in time to see a prairie dog stick its head out of a hole on the edge of their campsite. "Prairie dog!" she cried. Startled by her voice, the prairie dog popped back down its hole.

Josh was only too glad to get out of the moist tent, which was already heating up under the hot morning sun.

While the sleeping bags dried, the Reeds ate breakfast and watched the funny prairie dogs popping up all over. The prairie dog closest to them decided he was too close. He buried the hole entrance with himself inside as if to say, "I'm not here and neither is my hole.

After looking at prickly pear cactus and yucca and exploring the cliffs, the Reeds were ready to move on. They packed up the car, and that afternoon they crossed into New Mexico, the state where they would find the bat cave.

Chapter 8

The Bat Cave

The Reed family were the only people in sight in this desert for miles and miles. Josh could almost imagine they were the last people on earth, except for the wire fences and telephone lines that reminded him that people did live here somewhere.

This part of New Mexico looks pretty dry, Josh noticed. The only green things were yucca and other desert-type plants. Lots of sagebrush covered the land, but not trees. Every now and then he saw a lone bull or horse.

"Look!" Josh called. Dad saw them too and backed up the van for a better look. Mother and baby prong-horned antelope grazed beside the road.

Then they saw something else. It looked like a volcano rising from the desert-like prairie, but it was really a mountain named Haystack. *It must have reminded someone of a stack of hay,* Josh thought.

Then suddenly the land changed, and Josh marveled at the huge difference that water makes. With irrigation, the dry prairie had changed into green fields and small trees growing near houses. They were almost to Carlsbad, New Mexico.

That night they set up camp at White City. "Look what I found!" Isaac held something in his hands. It was a millipede with a lot of legs.

The next morning Isaac found something else while he and Josh were exploring near the camp. Isaac cried out.

"What's wrong?" Josh turned to his brother and saw it. A yucca thorn had gone deep into his leg.

"Hold on, Isaac," Josh said. "Mom! Dad! Help! Isaac's hurt!" Josh called.

Mom and Dad came running. "What happened?" Mom asked.

"It poked me," Isaac said through his tears as he pointed at the offending yucca plant.

Dad carefully picked up Isaac and carried him back to camp. Mom and Josh followed. The others came running. "Is Isaac okay?" they wanted to know.

"Let's take a look," Dad said. He set Isaac down and examined his leg. "All I can see is the hole, but I don't know if the thorn broke off inside. We should probably have a doctor take a look at it."

The Reeds found a hospital. While Dad took Isaac inside, Josh sat in the van with the others and prayed for his little brother. After a long wait, an exam, and two X-rays, the doctor decided that no thorn remained in Isaac's leg. He left with a Band-aid and a prescription for antibiotics in case his leg became infected. Everyone was so glad that Isaac was all right.

Finally, later that day, the Reeds reached Carlsbad Caverns and went into the visitor center to find out about tours.

"We are going down there?" Brittany asked doubtfully.

"That's why we're here," Will teased.

"But they said this walk through Carlsbad Caverns goes down eighty-three stories into the ground," Brittany said.

"This is going to be great!" Josh said. "Let's go!"

Down, down, down the family walked as they followed the lighted, paved trail that weaved farther and farther into the depths of the cave.

"What are those?" Isaac asked as he pointed to rock fingers sticking up from the ground.

"Those are stalagmites," Dad said. "The ones hanging down from the ceiling are stalactites."

"Look at that rock over there!" Will said.

The ranger smiled. "That is named Whale's Mouth."

As the ranger kept talking, Josh looked at the rock and decided that it did indeed look like a whale's mouth.

Will turned to Josh and Brittany. "Of course, this whole cave reminds me of a whale's mouth," he joked. "It is dark. Here we are inside and the stalactites and stalagmites look like teeth to me."

"Pretend what you want," Brittany said, "as long as we're not stuck in here for three days like Jonah."

"Let's see what's next," Ella said.

The Reeds kept walking and saw areas called the King's Palace, the Papoose Room, the Queen's Chamber, and the Big Room.

"This room is big. Imagine if we had a room in our house that was 8.2 acres," Josh said. "That's a little more than six football fields!"

"Hey, look," Ella said. "This rock formation doesn't have a name. Let's name it ourselves."

"How about Rocking Chair?" Brittany suggested.

"Or Stone-faced," Will said, "or Rock-a-bye Baby. Get it? *Rock*-a-bye? It's a rock."

The Reeds passed by a rock formation named Iceberg Rock and one spot called Bottomless Pit.

Brittany shivered. "Let's not get too close to that."

Still the path kept going. "Is this path ever going to end?" Brittany wondered out loud.

"I'm tired," Isaac said, "and my leg hurts."

"Come here, little brother," Will said as he swung Isaac up onto his back.

"We could pretend we're in a giant geode," Josh offered.

"That's better than imagining we're inside a whale," Brittany decided. "At least it's cool in here."

Finally, the Reeds came to the end of the trail, which left them deep under the ground. Thankfully, there was an elevator that took them back up to the surface.

"Daylight!" Mom declared as they stepped out of the cave. They had been underground for two and a half hours.

There was just enough time to eat dinner and watch the movie in the visitor center about bats.

At 7:30 p.m. the Reeds sat down with many others and waited for the Mexican free tail bats to come out of the cave.

Josh looked around. He practiced people-watching so he would be an even better detective or spy someday. It was then that he noticed someone watching them! A man to the right and behind them was taking a picture of his family!

"Dad!" Josh said. "A man just took our picture."

Dad shrugged. "He was probably just taking vacation pictures of the area and happened to have his camera pointing this direction. Besides, who would want a picture of this face?" Dad chuckled as he pointed to himself.

"I would, dear," Mom told him.

It was 7:50 p.m. "Look, the bats!" Isaac pointed to where a dark spiral of flying creatures rose higher and higher and then flew off in one direction. It reminded Josh of a swarm of bees he had once seen. The bats' exit lasted twenty minutes. There were a lot of bats.

That evening back at their campsite, it was time to read Nana's fifth clue. Dad opened the next envelope and read:

> **Sands** so **white** and very bright,
> but no beaches are in sight
> at this national monument.

Mom was looking through a guide of places to visit that listed national monuments. "Aha! I have this one," she exclaimed. "White Sands National Monument."

"They have a monument for sand?" Brittany asked doubtfully.

"I guess so," Mom said, smiling.

Josh wrote the clue and answer in his detective journal and then decided to write about the man who took their picture in his mystery 2 section. He wondered what would happen next.

Chapter 9

Sand Dunes

The next morning the Reeds crossed back into Texas again. A sign said "Salt Flats." "Let's stop here," Dad said as he found a place to park.

"But, Dad, I don't have any fries to go with all this salt," Will joked.

Josh stepped out of the van to look around. It reminded him of white sand, but when he tasted it, he knew it was definitely salt. The bright whiteness of the sun reflecting off the salt made his eyes water.

Josh and his family returned to the van and drove through the cactus-covered hills. Every now and then, Josh looked out the back window but saw no sign of anyone following them.

The next day the Reeds arrived at their destination, White Sands National Monument. Josh looked out the window at the white gypsum sand dunes that looked like snowy mountains around them. He could hardly wait to get out there.

As soon as the van stopped, Josh and Will scrambled out and quickly found that walking would be much more fun with no shoes. "Let's get rid of these!" Will said as he tossed his shoes back toward the van. Josh removed his shoes too and ran barefoot after Will through the cool white sand. They ran up to the top of a sand dune.

"Come on!" Josh called to the others.

Soon all of the Reeds were walking or running through the sand dunes. Isaac made it to the top of a sand dune and sat down. "Look what I can do!" he called as he slid down like he was riding a giant slide.

"That looks fun!" Brittany said and slid with Isaac.

Josh and Will went up and down another sand dune. When Will grinned that special "I've got a great idea" smile, Josh knew he was planning another scheme.

"Let me bury you," Will said.

"What?" Josh looked at his brother doubtfully.

"Then I'll call the others over to find you," Will explained.

"Okay," Josh agreed, "but I get to bury you too."

The two boys threw sand on each other and then wiggled their arms down into the sand until only their heads were showing. "Mom! Dad!" Will called.

Soon Mom and Dad appeared over the top of a dune. "Where are you?" Mom called.

"Down here," Josh said.

Mom looked surprised and then amused.

"Should we dig them out?" Dad asked her.

Mom seemed to be considering. "All I see are two heads, but since two heads are better than one, I think they can think of a way to get out."

"Good one, Mom," Will encouraged.

Josh and Will wiggled their arms free and then dug themselves out.

"Let's join Isaac and Brittany!" Josh said. The two raced off and slid down a dune by their sister and little brother. The sliding motion partly buried them again.

Dad decided to join the fun. He ran up a dune, but instead of sliding down, he opted to do a long jump. Through the air he sailed and landed softly in the sand.

"All right, Dad!" Will enthused.

"Let's try it!" Josh said excitedly.

Soon Josh, Will, Isaac, and Brittany, along with their dad, were taking flying leaps from the top of sand dunes and landing in the sand below. Mom and Ella decided they would rather not tumble around in the sand, so they watched and enjoyed the beautiful view of the Tularosa Basin.

Coming down a sand dune, Josh noticed something move. “Look, lizards!” he called.

Will flew through the air nearby. “Don’t you mean ‘Leaping Lizards’?” he yelled.

“No,” Josh tossed back. “I see lizards, but they are not leaping like you.”

Little lizards scooted away under a yucca as the kids approached.

The great lizard hunt had begun. Brittany spotted a blue lizard but it got away. The boys chased a brown lizard but did not get that one either. They refused to give up, though. They chased those lizards across the sand, between yucca and other plants. Eventually they returned with two white lizards which they showed to the others and then promptly let go. Later they bought rubbery white lizard souvenirs so they would always remember those fast little critters.

The Reeds waited to read Nana’s next clue until they had reached their next campsite. Josh could tell just by its name that his dad had chosen this place to camp: Rockhound State Park. Dad was definitely someone who liked to hunt for rocks. He was a real rockhound.

“We are here!” Dad said enthusiastically. The Reeds set up camp in a lovely spot among the cactus plants. Dad was eager to start exploring, but Josh really wanted to solve Nana’s next clue first. Dad opened and read the sixth clue:

> Isn’t it amazing? Isn’t it **grand**?
> **Can** you see **‘yon’** what was made by God’s hand?

“Can I try this one, Dad?” Josh asked.

Dad handed the note to Josh.

Josh quickly examined the clue. “Remember last time when Ella discovered that Nana put certain words in quotation marks to get our attention? It looks like she did something similar this time. Only instead of quotation marks, some words are darker.”

“Which words are boldfaced?” Dad asked.

“‘Grand,’ ‘can,’ and ‘yon’ are darker,” Josh replied. His face lit up. “Just put it together and it says Grand Canyon!”

“Where is the Grand Canyon?” Brittany wanted to know.

Mom pulled out the map. “Arizona.” She held the map closer so Brittany could take a look. “We will probably take this route,” Mom said as she pointed to the map.

“Now that we have that settled, is everyone ready to hunt for some gemstones?” Dad asked.

Josh jumped up excitedly. “Let’s go!”

Everyone moved to follow except for Mom. “I think I’ll stay here at the campsite this time,” she said. “That mountain you plan to climb looks steep. Have fun but be careful. God bless you and protect you.”

The others started up the long rocky trail, not knowing that soon one of them would be in deadly peril.

Chapter 10

Rockhounds and Canyons

"Look at this one!" Brittany held up a lovely piece of red jasper to show the others.

"That's great!" Josh looked back at his own growing rock pile. It had been a long, hard climb up the mountain near their campsite. Dad figured they had climbed about a mile, but it was worth it.

"Look at this one!" Josh called.

Dad came over to look. "This is perlite," Dad decided. "Nice."

"I've got something too, Dad," Will said.

Dad looked at Will's find. "Thunder eggs," he said. "These will look really smooth and shiny once we tumble them in our rock tumbler at home."

"Can I tumble mine too, Dad?" six-year-old Isaac asked hopefully.

"Of course," Dad replied. "Tumbling makes rocks smooth and shiny."

Ella stretched her back. "I think I have enough rocks. I'm ready to go back. Anyone want to come with me?"

No one else was ready to leave yet so Ella began the long descent down the mountain alone. In places she sat and slid down the path. In other places she jumped from one rock to another. As she carefully continued down, Ella thought of her sister, brothers, and dad and prayed that they would make it back safely too. Her prayers would be needed.

Will and Brittany soon returned to camp.

Finally, as it started to get dark, Josh, Isaac, and Dad started down the mountain.

Suddenly, Josh heard a rattling noise. He looked down in horror. Only eighteen inches from his feet, a gray and black splotched snake looked ready to strike.

With a quick reflex action, Josh immediately jumped sideways out of the way.

His dad was helping Isaac down a steep section of the trail, but Josh heard them coming. "Stop! Rattlesnake!" he cried out.

Dad froze in his tracks, grabbing Isaac's hand. "Where, Josh?"

"There." Josh pointed to the snake four feet in front of his dad and Isaac.

"Are you okay?" Dad asked.

Josh nodded.

"Thank You, Lord," Dad said.

"You can say that again," Josh agreed.

He did. "Thank You, Lord."

Josh breathed a sigh of relief as they watched the snake from a safe distance. Isaac, wanting to help his brother, threw a stone near the snake, which made it rattle more before it slithered away. Then Isaac ran over and hugged Josh, whose racing heart was just beginning to slow down.

Carefully, the three continued down the mountain. When they emerged from the semi-darkness, the others were glad to see them.

After they told the others what had happened, the family moved more cautiously around the dark campsite. "Maybe we should sleep in the car," Brittany suggested. "What if a rattlesnake comes in the tent and slithers into my sleeping bag?" She shuddered just thinking about it.

"We'll keep the tent zipped shut," Mom said, "and we can check our bedding for any snakes before we go to sleep. Okay?"

"Okay," Brittany sighed.

The Reed family did check for snakes that night. Unfortunately, they forgot something else.

Josh awoke to the sound of scraping noises outside the tent. "Dad, Mom," Josh whispered. "Something's out there." They did not wake up, so Josh quietly crawled to the tent door and slowly unzipped it just enough to peek out. He could see the black and brown furry bandits in the moonlight. Two raccoons were going through their food garbage. "Oh no!" Josh whispered.

"What is it, Josh?" Mom was awake now.

"Two raccoons are in our garbage," Josh replied quietly.

"We forgot to clean up after all the excitement," Mom remembered with dismay. She quietly lifted a flap and looked out a tent window. "Oh, that's not good."

"What?" Josh asked.

"A skunk is out there too." She called to it. "Go away, skunk!" The skunk did not care.

"Maybe we should quietly leave it alone and not get sprayed," Josh suggested.

"I guess that would be a good idea," Mom agreed. "Where would we sleep if our tent smelled like skunk?"

For a while, Josh watched the skunk out a tent window as it dug through the garbage and happily licked out cans. "There is nothing I can do about it," Josh decided, so he lay down again and tried to go back to sleep. Still, he could hear the noisy intruders pushing cans across the concrete floor near the picnic area.

Josh finally went to sleep only to be awakened again, not by sounds this time, but by a light shining outside the tent. His heart beat faster. The light was coming closer. Would he finally see the person that he thought was following them? He lifted up a flap to look out the tent window and saw a flashlight and the form of a man. As the person unzipped the tent door, Josh grabbed his own flashlight. Maybe he could use his flashlight as a weapon or at least shine it in the intruder's eyes.

A light shone into the tent. "Sorry, Josh. Did I wake you up?" It was the voice of his dad.

Josh sank back onto his sleeping bag with relief, but also with a little disappointment. He had thought the mystery would be solved, but now he realized that would not happen yet.

"I must have drunk too much water before bed," Dad explained. "The night life out here is exciting, though. I saw lots of ants and a kangaroo rat."

As Josh tried to settle back into sleep, he heard Will whisper to him, "Josh, why are you so worried about lights shining at night?"

"I really think someone is following us, Will," he answered.

"I have something to confess," Will said sheepishly. "Remember that day when you heard noises in the woods? It was me."

"How could it be you?" Josh was confused. "You were standing there with me."

"I know, but when you weren't looking, I threw some rocks into the woods. Those were the thumps that you heard."

"But why?" Josh asked.

"I just wanted to give you a mystery to solve," Will said. "I wasn't trying to scare you. I'm sorry."

It's okay, Will," Josh said, "but what about those flashes of light? Did you make those?"

"Well, no," Will admitted.

"And what about the guy who took our picture, and the black car?"

"Those could have logical explanations," Will told his brother. "Think about it. Why would anyone want to follow us? We are certainly not rich or famous."

"I know," Josh said. "I just have this hunch that all of these things are connected."

Will yawned. "Right now, I need to connect with my pillow and get some sleep. Goodnight, Josh."

"Goodnight, Will."

Chapter 11

In the Zone - Arizona

The next morning Josh awoke to the sound of Isaac calling, "Look at the ears on this rabbit!"

Josh was really tired, but he crawled to the tent opening and peered out. A young jackrabbit with big ears and a twitching nose had entered the campsite area. Isaac tried to sneak up on it, but the rabbit always stayed a safe distance away. Ella and Isaac followed it for a while before returning to camp.

After breakfast, Dad and Will wanted to look for more rocks, and Isaac wanted to look for cows. Some cattle were grazing nearby, and Isaac really wanted to pet one. Josh went with his little brother to get closer to the cows, but like the jackrabbit, the cattle were not interested in being petted either. When the boys walked toward them, the cattle moved away.

Then Josh saw it. An old black bull with horns bellowed at them.

He stopped. "Uh oh," Josh said. "Lord, please don't let this bull charge at us."

"What's wrong?" Isaac asked.

"I don't think that bull likes us here. Time to back away and head toward camp," Josh told his little brother.

"Should we run?" asked Isaac.

"Not yet," said Josh, "but I'll keep you posted."

The boys backed away and returned to camp. The bull did not charge.

When Isaac told Mom about the bull, Mom shook her head. "You are certainly keeping your guardian angels busy on this trip. Please stay close to camp and watch out for rattlesnakes too."

They did stay close and got a nice picture of a barrel cactus.

As the Reeds were packing up to leave, the wind whipped around and made a little dust twister about as tall as their dad. Around and around the wind spun, picking up dust and Dad's straw hat too. "Hey!" Dad yelled as he tried to grab his hat. After a good long chase, he returned with his hat.

On the road again and still in New Mexico, the Reeds crossed the Continental Divide. Dad explained it like this: "Before, if you poured some water on the ground, it would have headed toward the Atlantic Ocean. Now if you pour water on the ground, it will go the other way and end up in the Pacific Ocean."

The Reeds crossed into Arizona and through some of the Rocky Mountains. Josh was surprised that the mountains here were broken up with flatter areas.

Mom had a travel book open in her lap. "I think we should visit the Saguaro National Park while we're here."

"What is a saguaro?" Josh asked.

"It is a large tree-sized cactus. Listen to this." Mom read, "Saguaros usually grow to a height of thirty feet although sometimes they reach a height of fifty feet. They may live for two hundred years. Birds use these cactuses as homes. The saguaro blossom is the state flower of Arizona. Saguaros only grow in southern Arizona, southeastern California, and northwestern Mexico."

The Reeds decided to stop at the visitor center and watch a film about saguaros. Since they were the only ones in there, Will made his hand look like a shadow puppet on the screen. His hand looked like a talking head as Will opened and shut his hand to match the voice on the film. It was great fun, but they also learned that in the mountains above the saguaros, pine trees grow and snow falls in the winter.

Then the Reeds drove through the Saguaro National Park where they stopped to take pictures. "The saguaros almost don't look real," Josh said. They look like something in a cartoon." Suddenly, something zipped in front of them and ran across the road, living up to its name.

"Roadrunner!" Dad pointed and yelled excitedly.

Josh laughed. "Now I really feel like I'm in a cartoon!"

The roadrunner jumped up into a mesquite tree with bean-like pods and took a rest before running off again. "Beep, beep!" Will called. "Where's coyote?"

Isaac looked around nervously.

Will ruffled Isaac's hair. "I'm just joking," he said.

Everyone was so excited to see the roadrunner. As they drove through the saguaros, they were pleasantly surprised to see two more roadrunners in a little tree. "Three roadrunners in one day," Josh said happily.

When they saw tarantula holes, Josh, Will, and Isaac tried to fish the large spiders out of their holes with a piece of grass, but without success.

After a long tiring day, the Reeds set up camp in southern central Arizona and went to the pool for a swim. The pool was already occupied by four kids. Their mom and dad were sitting by the side, watching as the two boys and two girls tossed a beach ball back and forth. None of them were speaking English.

Ella slipped into the pool and asked the older girl, "Habla inglés?" (Do you speak English?)

"No," said the girl. "Habla español?" (Do you speak Spanish?)

"Un poco," (a little) Ella said modestly. Ella turned to her brothers and sister. "Come on. You can practice the Spanish you've been learning and make some new friends."

Will and Josh said "Hola" to say hello and started playing ball with the boys.

Dad and Mom had already started talking to the children's parents.

Brittany and Ella enjoyed the cool water as they talked with the girls. Although their Spanish was not perfect, Brittany and Ella learned that the family was on vacation from Mexico City where their dad was a doctor.

Ella could understand the Mexican family better than anyone else, so she listened as the Spanish-speaking mom explained what she wanted them to know. She told Ella that she had been watching the Reed family and was impressed with the closeness, the unity, the kindness she saw in their family. She did not see that unity in most American families.

Ella told the others what she had said. Then Ella tried to explain to the woman, "Somos Cristianos y esto es importante." (We are Christians and this is important.)

The woman smiled and nodded.

That evening after supper as Ella and Brittany discussed meeting their new Mexican friends, a sharp stinging pain caused Ella to cry out.

"What's wrong?" Brittany asked in alarm.

"My foot!" Ella said. "I think something stung me."

Dad hurried over with a lantern. He shone the light on the foot and surrounding area.

"It feels like bee stings down the side of my foot," Ella said.

"It does seem to be swelling and turning red," Dad observed.

They looked around but did not find what had bitten or stung her. Finally, Dad decided it was probably some ants. Although sore, her foot looked like it would be okay.

That night when most of the Reeds were asleep, another flash of light caused Josh to turn to Will. "Are you awake?" Josh whispered.

"I am," Will whispered back.

"Did you see the flash this time?" Josh asked.

"I did. Maybe it is a little strange," Will acknowledged. "But nothing bad has happened."

"You're right. Maybe we should ignore it and go to sleep. I am so tired," Josh yawned.

"We'll need lots of energy when we reach the Grand Canyon tomorrow," Will said. "Goodnight, Josh."

"Goodnight, Will."

As the Reeds were getting ready to leave their campsite the next morning, something scurried under Josh's shoe. "Ah!" Josh said and jumped back.

Will came over. "What is it?"

"Look," Josh said. "That is one major bug!"

The large bug scurried under Will's shoe.

"What's going on?" Isaac asked.

Will jumped back and the bug raced under Isaac's shoe.

Isaac ran for Dad with the bug in hot pursuit. Dad picked up Isaac. "I think that bug is just looking under your shoe for smaller insects to eat, or maybe it's looking for a place to hide. It won't hurt you."

The boys had fun running around while the bug chased them and looked under their shoes. Soon, though, it was time to head for the Grand Canyon and their highest adventure yet.

Chapter 12

Airplane Adventure

"We should arrive at the Grand Canyon today," Dad announced. Cheers erupted from the back seats.

"First, though, let's stop and visit the homes of some missing people," Dad said.

"Who is missing?" Josh asked.

"The Sinaguas," Dad said. "It actually happened a long time ago. These people were skilled in building, making jewelry, and using irrigation, but after three hundred years they mysteriously disappeared."

The Reeds saw a sign that said Montezuma Castle National Monument.

"Here we are," Dad announced.

"Everyone climbed out to look at the cave dwellings where the Sinaguas had lived. Josh wondered about the mystery. Had they all moved somewhere else? Was there a plague? Where had they gone? Josh figured this was one mystery that happened too long ago for him to solve. Besides, he still had mysteries of his own to solve.

Josh continued to think as they drove through Arizona's changing landscape. After driving through saguaros in the desert, they reached a place with small trees. In one spot,

Josh could really see the difference that water made. On one side of the road Josh saw desert, but on the other side irrigation allowed cotton fields with white fluffy balls to grow.

Elevation made a big difference too. Down low it was a hot desert, but as the car climbed up past the small trees into Ponderosa pine forests, the air became cooler and wetter. Then the road took them back down to an area with small trees again.

As they drove along, Dad suddenly cried, "Badger!" He slowed and tried to turn around.

"Watch out!" Mom cried.

In his excitement, Dad had accidentally driven off the road and into the grass. Everyone saw and admired the badger.

"Cool badger, Dad. Are we stuck?" Josh asked.

"Don't badger him, Josh." Will grinned at his own joke.

"Let's find out," Dad said. With a little effort, Dad was able to get the van back on the road and they continued on their journey.

The rest of the drive went smoothly, and finally the Reeds saw the Grand Canyon for the first time. They parked the van and walked to the edge.

"Not too close," Mom cautioned as she held Isaac's hand firmly.

"It's beautiful!" Brittany breathed.

"It's huge!" Will said.

Josh looked at the breathtaking view. "I'm glad that Nana got us to come here."

"Seeing pictures on TV is not the same as actually being here," Ella agreed.

That night the Reeds set up camp in the Kaibab National Forest near the Grand Canyon. It was beautiful and cool camping under the Ponderosa pines.

After breakfast, the Reeds returned to the Grand Canyon. "We have a surprise for you," Dad announced. "You are going to see more of the Grand Canyon from a different angle."

"Are we riding mules into the canyon?" Will asked.

Dad shook his head. "No."

"Good," Brittany said. "I like riding horses but not down into huge canyons."

"You are not going down," Dad explained, "but up!"

"Up?" Josh asked. "How can we go up? We are already at the top of the canyon, looking down."

"Let's take a drive," Dad said.

The Reeds drove until they saw airplanes.

"Of course!" Josh exclaimed. "We are going to fly over the canyon!"

It would cost quite a bit, but Mom and Dad said that this was a once-in-a-lifetime opportunity. Then all of them boarded the little plane.

Josh sat near a window, his eyes glowing with excitement as the plane started to move. Faster and faster it went until Josh felt it leave the ground. As the plane climbed, it bumped, making Josh's insides rise and fall. After the plane was up in the air, though, and flying straight, the ride smoothed out and Josh could concentrate on the view.

Over the trees they flew, and Josh watched as the land dropped away. They were over the canyon. It was so big that the plane seemed to be inching along slowly even though it was really going quite fast. The canyon seemed to rise and fall, and Josh could see the blue-green Colorado River snaking its way through the canyon.

It seemed like a good time to take pictures. Isaac, Brittany, Will, and Ella had already been snapping pictures left and right. Josh took a picture and then saw something glinting in the sunlight on the edge of the canyon.

Josh pulled out his binoculars for a closer look. It was a man taking a picture of them! Josh nudged Will. He handed

the binoculars to him and pointed to where sunlight still reflected off the camera lens of the man taking their picture.

Will gazed through the binoculars and nodded to Josh. They would talk later.

For now, the plane was taking them farther away, and Josh's stomach was feeling uneasy. The bumping and jostling were upsetting his stomach. About halfway through the trip, Josh started saying to himself, "I am not going to throw up. I am not going to throw up. I am not going to throw up. Please, God, I don't want to throw up on this plane."

Josh's stomach did not appreciate the bumpy descent back down to the airport, but he did not throw up. He was very glad to walk around and let his stomach calm down.

He found Will. "So what do you think?" Josh asked.

"It did look like that man was taking our picture," Will said.

"But why would he take our picture?" Josh wondered.

"Maybe he just wanted the plane in the picture for scale so it would show how big the canyon was in comparison," Will suggested.

"Maybe," Josh acknowledged. "But I think our picture is being taken too many times to just be a coincidence."

"You are starting to convince me, Josh," Will said.

Back in their van again, the Reeds drove from one spot to another along the canyon's rim. It was hot, but what a view!

At one of these stops, Dad suggested, "Let's read Nana's next clue."

"Good idea." Mom sat down and fanned herself.

The Reed family gathered around as Dad opened and read the seventh clue:

> Don't let the "sun set"
> before you see this "crater,"
> or is it a "volcano"?

Mom pulled out a travel guide and map.

"This is a hard one," Josh said.

"Can I see the clue, Dad?" Will asked.

Will looked at the clue. "Well, 'sun set' is in quotation marks. So is 'crater' and 'volcano.' Is there something called Sunset Crater Volcano?"

"Yes, there is," Mom smiled and said, "and we are not far away. In fact, if we left now, we might arrive before dark."

The Reeds excitedly climbed back into the van. Before long, they saw a sign that said only twenty-seven miles to Sunset Crater Volcano.

Chapter 13

Lava Tubes

The park was full, but the Reeds were given permission to camp in the national forest. "Let's fill our water jugs first," Mom said.

After getting the needed water, the Reeds drove into the forest. "What a view!" Josh said. The road was taking them right past Sunset Crater Volcano at sunset.

"Let's camp here," Dad suggested.

As the Reed kids set up the tent, Josh looked around and knew that he would never forget this campsite. They were camping right in the black cinders of Sunset Crater Volcano! "I hope it doesn't erupt," Josh commented.

"This volcano has been dormant a long time. We are completely safe—at least from erupting volcanoes," Dad said.

That night both Josh and Will saw a flash of light and scrambled to unzip the tent flap and peer out. They were just in time to see a dark figure disappear into the trees.

"Boys," Dad called sleepily. "Is everything all right?"

"We both saw a flash of light, Dad," Will said, "and it looked like someone was out there."

"I'll take a look," Dad said as he climbed out of his sleeping bag. He grabbed a flashlight and slipped on his shoes at the tent entrance.

In five minutes he was back. "I didn't see anything," Dad informed the boys. "Let's try to get some sleep."

Who had been out there? Josh wondered, and what was that flash of light? Josh was still thinking about it when he fell asleep.

The next morning, though, all thoughts of the night before had disappeared. It was time to explore the area around what used to be an active volcano!

Dad led the way. "That is the cinder cone with the crater way up there," he explained. "Feel this." Dad gave them some light cinders. Then they felt some basalt. Josh could feel that the sharp lava stones were much heavier than the cinders.

"What is this?" Josh asked as he pointed to what looked like a tunnel.

"It's a lava tube," Dad explained. "The hot lava flowed this way. The outside of the lava cooled first and hardened while the lava inside kept flowing farther, so a tube was formed."

"Cool!" Josh said. "Let's follow it."

The Reeds followed the lava tube to see where the lava had flowed. They saw that the tube had partially collapsed so it had holes in it and flattened areas.

"I have a better idea," Will said. "Instead of following it from up here, let's go into the lava tube!"

"I don't know if that's a good idea," Mom said with concern.

"We'll be careful," Will said.

"What do you think, Dan?" Mom asked Dad.

"It should be okay. I'll even go with them," he assured her.

"Oh, all right," Mom conceded, "but be careful."

Will, Josh, Isaac, Brittany, and Dad climbed down the holes into the lava tubes, but Brittany came back. "The rocks are too sharp," she explained.

Mom and the girls could hear Dad and the boys inside the cave-like lava tube. Occasionally, they could even see them through holes as they followed them from above.

"This is so cool," Josh said as he climbed through the lava tube. Sunlight came in through the holes and cracks so it was easy to see, but it still felt like a cave.

"This way looks a little tight, but I'll try to get through," Josh told the others. "Oh, uh, I can't go any farther," he groaned. Josh had tried to push his way through a collapsed part of the tunnel, but now he realized that had not been a good idea. "Hey, guys, I'm stuck!"

He heard Will's voice. "Hold on. I'll just pull you back." Will grabbed his legs and started to pull.

"Ow! Stop! The rocks are sharp. They're scraping my stomach!" Josh cried out.

Josh could hear worried voices above him.

"Okay, Josh, can you carefully move yourself back?" Dad asked.

Josh tried to wiggle. "No, I think my pants or shirt are caught on something."

"Okay, Josh, don't panic. Lord, please show us what to do here," Dad prayed. He thought a moment. "I'm going to try to reach under you and find what you are caught on," Dad said. "Can you lift your stomach up at all?"

"I'll try," Josh said.

Dad struggled to find a way to get Josh unstuck. "I think your belt loop is stuck on a piece of rock. If I can just lift the loop off…" Dad brought his hand back.

"Okay, Will. Let's pull Josh back slowly," he said.

Josh began to move backwards. It was working!

Josh, Will, Isaac, and Dad felt they had enough lava tube excitement and climbed out to see Mom, Ella, and Brittany, who also felt that they had enough lava tube excitement. Mom got out the first aid kit to clean and cover the scrapes on Josh's stomach. Josh was surprised to see the back of Dad's hand bleeding. Dad just shrugged and smiled. "It's okay, Josh. We had to get you out." Even Will and Isaac had a few scrapes and cuts from the sharp lava rocks.

After everyone was cleaned up, Mom got out Nana's clues. "I think it's time to read clue number eight. Why don't I read this one while you let your hand recover, Dan."

Dad agreed. Then Mom had an idea. "Isaac, can you open the United States map for me? You can help solve this clue while I read. Here it is:

> Can you be in four states at the same time? You can try here.

"Look at the map, Isaac. Do you see a place where four states all touch in one corner?" Mom asked.

Isaac looked and looked. Finally, he smiled and poked the map with his finger. "Here it is!"

"Good job, Isaac," Mom said. "Four corners, here we come!"

Chapter 14

Four Corners

Josh looked out the window and saw a sign about the Four Corners National Monument.

The van slowed down. “Here we are!” Dad called to the back.

“Woo-hoo!” Will rushed out. He ran up the steps to where the corners of the four states were marked on a bronze disk set in a granite floor. Josh and the others followed.

Josh thought Will looked like he was playing Twister.

“Look at me!” Will said. “My right hand is in Colorado, my left hand is in Utah, my right foot is in New Mexico, and my left foot is in Arizona. I feel so mixed up.”

Will pulled himself out of three states and gave Josh a turn.

Josh stood right in the middle, with his feet touching all four states. “I did it! I stood in four states at the same time!”

Josh moved back and noticed Brittany had a silly smile on her face as she moved toward the four corners. Suddenly, she was on her head. “Look! I can do a headstand in four states at the same time.”

Now Ella had an idea. As she got to where the four states met, she started dancing. "I can dance in four states at the same time!"

Isaac wanted a turn. "See? I can jump in four states at the same time!"

Not to be left out, Dad stood on the four states' corners and cupped his hands around his mouth. "Yo de lay, yo de lay, yo de lay he hoo!" he called.

"Dad," everyone groaned.

"What? I just wanted to yodel in four states at once," he said with sparkling eyes.

It was Mom's turn, but she was still thinking. Then she smiled. "I know what to do. Josh, could you time me on your stopwatch please?"

"Sure, Mom," Josh answered. Mom stood near the four corners in New Mexico.

"Go!" said Josh.

Mom ran a quick circle around the four corners. "Stop!" she called. "How long was that?"

"Four seconds," Josh told her.

"Good, now I can say that I ran through four states in four seconds."

"That's great, Mom!" Will could appreciate that.

The Reeds returned to the van and settled back to hear Nana's next clue.

"Actually, it looks like two clues go together," Dad said as he pulled out an envelope labeled "Clues 9 and10." "How can we go to two places at the same time?" he wondered aloud.

Josh had a thought. "Maybe it's like this place where you can be in four places at once."

Dad read the ninth clue:

> Don't be <u>scared</u> of these <u>woods</u>.
> The trees have all turned to stone.

It was a strange clue. At first no one said anything. They were all busy thinking.

Then Brittany asked, "Are any of the words in the clue in quotation marks?"

"No, but two words are underlined," Dad said. "'Scared' and 'Woods.'"

Brittany looked puzzled. "I've never heard of scared woods before."

Josh had an idea. "Maybe it's something *like* those words. Another word for woods could be forest." He thought a minute. "'Scared forest' doesn't make sense either, though."

"What's the rest of the clue?" Will asked.

Dad read, "The trees have all turned to stone."

"I remember reading about that. Stone trees, stone forest," Will thought aloud. Suddenly, he slapped the back of the seat. "I've got it! Petrified is another way to say 'scared' and it can mean 'turned to stone.' It's the Petrified Forest!"

"Good job," Dad congratulated. "That was a tough clue. It took three people to figure it out, but you did it together."

"We still have another clue, though," Mom said. "Ella and Isaac, do you want to try this one?"

Ella looked at Isaac and smiled. "We can try."

Dad handed the tenth clue to Ella. She read, "What is a colorful dessert without one 's'?"

"Look, Isaac. The words 'colorful dessert' are underlined. Let's take out one 's' from 'dessert.'"

Isaac crossed it out.

"Now it says 'desert,'" Ella told him.

"We're going to a desert," Isaac announced happily.

"Good job, but which one?" Ella wondered. "A colorful desert. I know! The Painted Desert!"

Mom looked at the map. "I've found it." She pointed at the map. "Right here is the Petrified Forest National Park and the Painted Desert in the same place."

Josh wrote down the clues and answers in his detective journal under the section entitled "Treasure Hunt." He also had a map of the United States so he could mark each stop and keep track of where they were. A separate section entitled "Mystery?" was growing with more strange occurrences such as a man running away, someone taking their picture, and being followed by a black car. Next to his columns of "What happened" and "Where," he had added "Why" and "Who." Yes, this definitely looked like a second mystery, Josh thought.

The Reeds stopped to visit a Hogan, an eight-sided house, and walked inside. The Hogan was made of wood, mud, and sticks. Still, Josh had an uneasy feeling of being watched even as they visited the Canyon de Chelly and saw the ruins of the pueblos and cave dwellings of the Anasazi, ancestors of modern Native American tribes. Maybe looking at the clues in his journal had made him feel this way, Josh decided. After all, why would anyone be watching them?

Chapter 15

Petrified

As they drove, Dad cupped his hand by his mouth to direct his words to the back. "Next stop, Petrified Forest National Park and Painted Desert!"

At the visitor center, everyone watched a movie about petrification and learned how the wood had been replaced with stone. Going back to the car, Josh suddenly stopped as stone still as the petrified wood they had come to visit. Will accidentally ran into him. "Oof! Uh, Josh, keep moving, or someone might take a picture of petrified Josh!"

Josh stood silently.

"Get it?" Will tried again. "You're not moving, you're still like a stone, like the Petrified Forest? Josh?"

"It's the car," Josh finally said.

"What car?" Will asked.

"Remember I thought someone was following us? Well, I wrote down the license plate number from the car back in Missouri. This is it! The same car! I can prove it now!"

Josh and Will ran over to where their dad was just unlocking their van door. They explained the strange car sighting.

"Hmm," Dad said, giving it some thought. "It is strange. Still, maybe the owner of that car just happens to be going the same way that we are."

When the boys began to protest, Dad held up his hand. "I know, I know. The fact that the car is here does bear watching. Let's just wait and see if it turns up near us again. We'll keep our eyes open."

The Reeds drove around, stopping often to see the stone logs. They had learned that a long time ago the logs had been buried under many layers of soil and rocks and then replaced by silica to form exact replicas of the original wood logs. Then as the land pushed upward, the stone logs had come to the surface and broken into pieces of various lengths.

"It looks so strange," Brittany said, giggling. "There are no trees, just logs lying around, and the logs look like someone came along and cut them into firewood-length pieces." She touched one. "But when you feel one, you can tell that it's stone, not wood now."

"Oh, look, the sun came out!" Ella exclaimed. The lovely reds and purples of the beautiful, layered Painted Desert were glorious in the sunlight. Ella held up her camera and motioned everyone closer together. "Quick, let's get a picture while the sun is shining on it."

Everyone smiled and said "cheese" except for Will, who said, "Petrified Trees!"

"Where are we going next?" Josh wanted to know.

"Let's take a look," said Dad. He took Nana's next clue out of his pocket and read clue number eleven:

> Is it a bird? Is it a plane?
> No, but something flew through the air
> and made this crater. Watch out for meteors!

"Wherever we are going, it sounds great!" Josh exclaimed. "The clue says there is a crater, but what about meteors? Did a meteor really make a crater around here?"

Mom had gone to the car for a map. Now she studied it. "Good work, Josh. Here it is, Meteor Crater."

Just then a vibrant rainbow appeared against the dark sky. "Ooh! Look!" Brittany exclaimed.

"Now it looks like God painted the desert and the sky," Isaac decided.

"It really does," Mom agreed.

That evening Josh and his brothers and sisters were thrilled to see a swimming pool at their campsite. Before he swam, though, Josh wrote down Nana's clue in his detective journal and the answer. If only he had an answer to the mystery as well.

The next day Dad bought some petrified wood and they visited some buffalo. Then they were on their way.

Meteor Crater in Arizona was the first stop of the day. Ella got out and shivered in her T-shirt and shorts. "I thought it was going to be hot again today."

Brittany agreed. "I know, it was hot back at camp this morning, but now it is cloudy, cold, and starting to rain."

"I've got a song for the occasion!" Will cried with glee.

"Oh no!" the girls said in unison.

Will started singing "Oh Susanna," and Josh joined in. As they sang about the rain and dry, hot and froze, the girls thought it was funny and decided to join in too.

The Reeds entered the visitor center first and warmed up while they looked at some meteor pieces. "Look at this meteorite fragment that someone found!" Josh told the others. "It says this meteorite piece weighs 1,406 pounds!"

Then they walked outside into the cold rain. "That is one huge hole in the ground!" Will exclaimed. It was an impressive crater–over 4,000 feet across and 550 feet deep.

"I wonder if we will ever see one hit the earth during our lifetime," Brittany said.

"Just be glad you were not standing here when this one hit," Will teased.

Mom was looking cold. "Let's get out of this rain."

Back in the van, they were ready to read Nana's twelfth clue. Josh got out his detective journal. Dad looked puzzled. This clue says, "Psalm 23:4 NIV 12th word, 7th word."

Ella pulled out her Bible. "I've got it, Dad." She began to read. "Even though I walk through the valley of the shadow of death, I will fear no evil, for you are with me; your rod and your staff, they comfort me."

Josh wrote down Psalm 23:4 under his clue category. "What's the twelfth word?" he asked.

Ella counted. "Death."

"That does not sound promising," Will said.

"Yeah, are we really going someplace called 'Death'?" Brittany asked.

"Maybe we should count again," Mom suggested.

Ella counted the words in the verse again. "The twelfth word is death and the seventh word is valley. Death Valley."

Josh wrote the answer in his journal. "Well, the verse says God is with us even in the valley of the shadow of death, so let's go!"

The Reeds drove out of the rain, but not out of Arizona yet. They were in western Arizona now in the Mojave Desert.

Isaac pointed out the window at a desert tree with sharp-looking leaves. "What's that?" he asked.

Let's find out," Mom said. She looked in a book and found it. "It's a Joshua tree."

"Can we stop?" asked Will. "I need a picture of that."

Dad pulled over beside the road, and Will hopped out. "Come on, Josh," he called back.

Josh looked confused. "What? Me?"

"Of course," Will said, grinning. "I need a picture of Joshua in a Joshua tree."

"Oh, brother," Josh groaned, but then again, climbing the cactus-looking tree did look fun. Soon Josh was in a Joshua tree. Isaac and Will climbed up in Joshua trees too.

The others decided to look around while they waited. "Notice the tumbleweed!" Dad called in his best tour guide voice. Brittany felt the stiff, scraggly tumbleweed. That is when she saw it.

Something had moved. Thinking it was a big spider, she carefully watched the bush where it hid. To her surprise, it was not a spider. "Look what I found!" Brittany called. "I think it's a little lizard."

Dad came over and caught it. "Why, it's a baby horny toad. How cute."

Brittany was not sure about the cute part.

The Reeds searched the area for more. "I've got one!" Will called.

"Me too!" Josh called back. They returned to the group so everyone could hold them and take pictures. Then they let them go.

It was time to move on. As the Reeds drove out of Arizona, Josh wondered what lay in store in Death Valley.

Chapter 16

Death Valley

The Reeds left Arizona on Hoover Dam and entered Nevada. It was getting dark, but they still got out of the van and walked on the impressive dam containing the Colorado River. They could see the river far below.

Driving on, they found a campsite at Lake Meade. It was warm but not like it would be tomorrow, Josh knew. Soon they would be in the hottest place in the United States–Death Valley.

The next day, it was on to California and into Death Valley. The Reeds stopped. The heat was incredible, Josh thought. He looked at the thermostat on the car. It was 115 degrees in the shade!

There are adventures to be had even in Death Valley. The Reeds, wearing hats and sunscreen for protection against the hot glaring sun, began searching for the elusive pupfish. "Uh, Dad, I don't see any water around here," Will said.

"There used to be a large lake here long ago," Dad explained.

That's hard to believe now, Josh thought. It looked so dry. After walking a long way on a boardwalk, they eventually found a puddle.

"I see them!" Isaac said excitedly. Sure enough, small, silvery pupfish swam in the puddle.

"Here in the Mojave and Sonoran deserts may be the only place in the world where this species of fish exists," Dad remarked.

A desert seems like a funny place to find fish, Josh thought.

Back in the car again, Josh looked out the window at the barren land. Not much was growing here, Josh noticed. Some parts of Death Valley looked like flat brown land, other parts looked like dry rocky hills, and other parts looked like sand dunes. *No wonder they call it Death Valley,* Josh thought. Things looked dead. It was so hot and dry.

"Can we stop and get some pictures of these sand dunes?" Will asked.

"I want to get some pictures too," Brittany said.

Dad stopped the van. How could they have known what would happen next?

Cameras in hand, Will, Brittany, Josh, Isaac, and Dad hopped out. There were no boardwalks here, just hot burning sand. Mom and Ella said that it was too hot and decided to stay in the van.

As the others walked out into the sand dunes and started taking pictures, they realized that this was the hottest sand they had ever encountered. "Ow, Ow, Ow!" Isaac cried out.

"What's wrong?" Dad asked.

"The sand hurt my foot," Isaac told him.

"He must have gotten some sand in his shoe." Dad picked him up, and Will dumped a little sand out of Isaac's shoe. His foot looked slightly red.

Dad was just about to carry Isaac back to the car when he stumbled and looked down. "Dad, your shoe fell apart," Josh noticed.

Dad shook his head in amazement. "The hot sand actually melted the glue holding my shoe together!"

Now they needed a new plan to get back to the van. Will carried Isaac on his back. Brittany and Josh helped their Dad hop back to the van with his one remaining shoe.

Only their troubles were not over yet. The air conditioner had been running and the van had overheated. They were stranded in Death Valley!

"What are we going to do?" Brittany wailed.

"We're not going to panic," Mom said in a calm but serious tone.

Josh looked down the road in both directions even though he knew it would probably be a long time before anyone else would drive along this deserted stretch of road. Nothing.

"Dad, what about your cell phone," Josh asked.

"Good thought," Dad responded as he pulled out the phone. After a minute, though, he sighed. "It's not working."

Dad ran his hands over his face in a nervous gesture. "At least we have water. We will sit and wait for the engine to cool. Then I'll add some water, and we'll pray we make it to the next town."

The Reeds rolled down the windows so the sun would not heat the van to an even hotter temperature than the outside air. Then they drank from their water bottles and waited. No one said much as the minutes ticked by.

Then it was time. Dad added some water, prayed, and started the van. It worked! Before long, they arrived in a little town.

The Reed family had never been so glad to get out of the van. As Josh entered the General Store, he took a big breath of the cool air while Will joyfully cried, "Air conditioning!"

The Reeds bought some packaged cookies, chips, and drinks. As they munched, they cooled off in the store. Twenty minutes later, Dad assembled the group and said, "Now we have to drive up and out of Death Valley."

The kids groaned. Even Mom was reluctant to leave the cool store, but it had to be done.

They were in the van again. To take everyone's mind off their present difficulties, Ella read a chapter from an adventure novel to everyone. Of course, Josh knew they were living their own adventure right now.

Higher and higher the van climbed out of Death Valley. It was so hot. They knew that turning on the air conditioner could make the already stressed van overheat, so the air conditioner stayed off. No one complained because no one wanted to be stranded in Death Valley again.

The engine light came on anyway. The Reeds stopped the van and waited for the engine to cool. "Look!" Dad pointed. "A chuckwalla!" Everyone scrambled to see the large lizard.

"Cool!" Will said.

"You mean hot," Josh quipped.

"Well, yeah," Will agreed, "but the chuckwalla is cool. Let's get a closer look."

Josh, Will, Brittany, and Isaac left the van and snuck toward the chuckwalla. The chuckwalla had other ideas. It ran, so the kids ran after it, but they soon gave up. It was too hot.

With everyone on board again, the Reeds continued the steep climb out of Death Valley. They had to stop yet again, but at least there was radiator water at different points along the road.

The next time the engine light turned on, they had almost made it out of Death Valley. Dad figured they were not in the national monument area anymore, so they collected lava rocks as state souvenirs.

The hot, tired family managed a weak "Hurray!" as they left Death Valley behind, but the difficult travel was not over yet.

Josh looked out the window and thought it still looked like a desert. Then through the mountains they went. As the van twisted and turned, Josh thought it was exciting to see places beside the road where it just dropped away in a cliff without even any guard rails to keep a vehicle from plunging over the edge. Mom did not think it was exciting. She thought it was dangerous. Josh could see her lips moving in prayer as she clutched the seat.

Up and down, up and down the road went, making Josh's ears pop and the engine get hot again. This time they stopped at a radiator water tank and refilled a lot of their containers.

It was 8:20 p.m. now and getting dark. "Mom, are we going to have supper?" Isaac wondered. "I'm hungry."

Josh's own stomach rumbled. They had eaten only cookies and salty chips today although they had drunk a lot of water to keep from getting dehydrated.

Not finding any places to eat, the Reeds stopped for water, directions, and ice cream on a stick. Mom and Dad decided that they should keep driving into the night. It was cooler now and the van would not overheat.

Josh tried to sleep but felt trapped in the hot, stuffy van. He turned this way and that way.

"What's wrong, Josh?" Brittany wanted to know.

"It just feels so closed in, stuffy, and hot. I want out," Josh admitted.

"Me too," Brittany agreed. "I have an idea. Just think about being back at home, standing on the hill beside our pond with the cool green trees blowing in the breeze."

That was one of Josh's favorite spots, so he closed his eyes and thought about the openness there. It helped. "Thanks, Brittany," Josh mumbled and fell asleep.

Around 11:00 p.m. the Reeds arrived at Red Rock Canyon State Park. Sleepily, they set up camp on the sand among the brush, rocks, and Joshua trees.

Although they were in bed by 12:30, they were up at 7:30 a.m. The hot sun had driven them out of their beds.

"Let's hope Nana's next clue sends us somewhere cooler," Will said.

"Let's read it now," Josh encouraged.

"I guess we should see where we are going," Dad agreed.

Everyone gathered around as Dad opened and read the thirteenth clue:

> On the top of a mountain,
> In a land of giants,
> These trees are the widest.

"I know this one," Dad said, "and it will be great."

"Where are we going?" Isaac asked.

Dad swung him up in the air. "To see giant trees so big you can go inside the trunks. Some say they are the largest living things. The giant sequoias!"

Chapter 17

Giants

They were not quite ready to leave camp yet. Josh and Will had seen a steep mountain near the campsite that they longed to explore. "We won't be long!" they called as they hurried toward the mountain that just begged to be climbed.

Loose gravel on the mountain made climbing difficult. Their feet kept sliding back down because of the loose stones, but slowly they made progress.

It was then that Josh heard loose stones falling behind them. When he turned around, he saw his little brother Isaac following them.

"Isaac, this is too dangerous. You need to go back to the camp," Josh said.

"But *you* are climbing up here," Isaac answered.

Josh was going to say, "Yeah, but I'm older," when he suddenly saw how far up they had come and wondered how they were going to get down safely. Maybe this had not been such a good idea after all.

"Hey, Will!" Josh called to his older brother. "Look down!"

Will did. "Wow, I guess we should start heading down now."

"Isaac followed us," Josh added. "We need to get all three of us down safely."

When Mom looked toward the mountain, she saw the three boys and immediately grew concerned. "Dan, Isaac followed them and is trying to climb that mountain too. It looks like they might be having trouble getting down."

"I'll get them!" Dad called as he sprinted toward the boys.

Will and Josh slowly backed down until they reached Isaac. "My feet keep slipping," Isaac said. "I don't know how to get down."

"We'll go first," Will told him. "That way if you fall, we'll catch you."

We hope, Josh thought.

"Whoa!" Will yelled. He slid three feet before catching himself. Josh leaned over to help steady him. "I'm okay," Will said.

Josh slid too, but Will steadied him.

When Isaac began to slide, Will and Josh held him up. Safely, they arrived at the bottom where their dad was waiting.

"Isaac, you did not ask our permission to go mountain climbing and could have gotten hurt, but we'll talk about that later," Dad said.

Dad turned to Will and Josh. "I'm not sure how wise it was to go that high, but I did see something good just now. You were working together, helping each other and Isaac. We do need to be there for each other and hold each other up, because in this life there will be difficulties you will face. We need God. We need each other. So remember this day when you kept each other from falling."

The Reeds drove out of the Mojave Desert, past many windmills, and through hilly golden grasslands. "The hills look like golden velvet," Brittany said, "or the material on our sofa when you brush it one way to make it a lighter color or the other way to make it a darker color."

They had driven into California's Central Valley and saw irrigated orange groves, grapes, and lots of other green, watered things.

Finally, they reached the visitor center for the sequoias. "Where are they?" Josh asked. Not a tree was in sight.

"I'll go see what I can find out," Dad said. He left the van and walked into the visitor center.

Josh was hot. *It must be over 100 degrees*, he thought.

Dad returned. "We have to drive up to see the sequoias."

"Up where?" Will asked.

"Up a mountain," Dad explained, "but it will be steep. We should leave our trailer here." The Reeds unhitched Explorer and returned to the van.

Up, up, up the van climbed on the winding roads. It twisted higher and higher. "I wonder if whoever made this road was following a snake at the time," Dad joked.

"Good one, Dad," Will said.

Josh noticed that Mom looked pale. That was probably because on one side the road hugged a mountain wall while on the other side the ground disappeared in a steep cliff. This drive was an adventure in itself.

The desert plants were giving way to small trees, Josh noticed. As they went higher, the temperature dropped. Still, they kept going up.

Now the small trees were being replaced by larger trees, and the temperature was in the 80s instead of over 100 degrees.

Then they were at the top. "Amazing!" Josh exclaimed as he saw that they were now above many of the mountains they had looked up at before.

"It's like a fairytale," Brittany breathed in awe. "You know, like Jack and the Beanstalk. We go way up high and find a giant world. If only there were a giant castle with kings and queens, princes and princesses."

"Fee, Fi, Fo, Fum," Will said in a deep voice. "It doesn't look like anything I've ever seen before. It's like we've stepped into a storybook."

As the Reeds walked around, they were truly amazed. One tree named General Sherman was at least thirty feet across at the base and over two thousand years old.

Will picked up a little cone on the ground. "It's hard to believe something so small can become so big. God is awesome."

"Look at the black area on this tree," Josh said.

"Some of these trees look like they have survived even fire," Dad said. "They are quite old."

"Take my picture here!" Brittany called as she stood in a crack of a tree. Josh did.

"Look at me!" Isaac called. "I'm inside a tree cave."

It did look like a cave inside a tree, Josh decided.

Then Josh saw a fearless mule deer that lay down beside a towering giant of a tree. The deer looked like a toy next to the giant sequoia. It would make a great picture.

Josh went closer to take its picture, but the deer stood up and casually strolled away. Josh decided to follow it and try to take its picture again, but the deer kept walking. Josh kept following.

Finally, the deer stopped. *At last!* Josh thought. He held up his camera. Click! He got the picture. Now he was ready to head back.

Josh turned around, but all he saw were more trees. Where were the others? He must have wandered farther than he thought. When he listened, all he heard were the peaceful sounds of the forest, but Josh felt anything but peaceful. Which way should he go? Maybe he should sit and wait and let the others find him so he would not accidentally wander farther away.

As he sat down, he heard a noise and jumped back up again. A stranger wearing dark sunglasses stepped out from behind a tree. "Are you lost?" he asked.

Josh did not know how to respond. He knew not to talk to strangers, but he was lost.

The man did not come any closer. He only pointed and said, "A family calling 'Josh' is that way."

"Thank you, sir!" Josh said and began to run in the direction that the man had indicated.

Soon he could hear his name being called. "Josh! Josh!"

Josh ran toward them. "I'm here!"

His family surrounded him in a group hug. "We were so worried!" Mom said.

Josh explained about the mule deer and the mysterious stranger.

Suddenly, Josh had a hunch. As they walked back to the van, Josh scanned the area until he found it. A black car was parked not far away. "Mom, Dad, could I go check the license plate on that car?" he asked.

"Okay, but I'm coming with you this time," Dad decided.

Josh grabbed his detective journal from their van, and they walked over to compare the numbers. The license plate numbers matched! "See, Dad, he *is* following us!" Josh said excitedly.

"This is strange," Dad admitted.

Dad and Josh returned to the van. Then the Reeds waited for the driver of the black car to return. "This is like being a spy in a novel," Will said as he hunched down low in his seat and peered out the window.

"I see someone coming," Brittany whispered loudly.

They watched as a man unlocked the door of the black car and got inside.

"That's him!" Josh exclaimed. "That's the man who helped me when I was lost!"

Chapter 18

Bears or Sharks?

Coming back down from the mountaintops, the Reeds felt the heat returning. To Josh, it seemed like they had come back down into the real world.

As he sat in the van, he wondered. *Who was that man? What did he want? Why did he help me like that?*

Josh had a mystery to solve, but right now it was time for Nana's fourteenth clue. Dad read:

> You have seen the widest, but have you seen the tallest?
> These trees are grand, the tallest in the land.

"You mean there are trees taller than the sequoias?" Brittany asked.

"I know!" Ella exclaimed. "The redwoods."

Finding the redwoods would have to wait until tomorrow. The Reeds hitched up the Explorer and drove to a campsite in the lower parts of the mountains that night.

It was almost dark, but Josh managed to read a sign that listed campsite rules. "Hey, guys, listen to what this sign says," Josh began. "Do not feed the wildlife..."

Will cut in, "But I'm hungry!"

"Not you," Josh returned. "It says, 'especially bears.' It also says, 'If a bear is sighted, clap and make noise to scare the bear away. Tell a park ranger.'"

"Maybe I'll sleep in the van tonight," Brittany said, shivering.

"We've been in other bear areas," Josh said, "and nothing has happened."

"But this place actually gets you ready to meet a bear," Brittany argued.

"Then you'll be ready," Josh said, grinning.

As they ate dinner, another camper stopped by and told them that five bears had wandered through the camp last night, including a mother and two cubs. Darkness had fallen. The Reeds quickly finished eating and put their food away so no wandering bears would join them for supper.

Everyone settled into the tent for the night. Tonight the tent seemed especially flimsy as Josh thought about bears, but he drifted off into an uneasy sleep.

Josh awoke suddenly to noise outside. Mom was already awake and peering out the tent window. "What is it?" Josh asked.

"Just some more campers coming in," Mom explained. "Goodnight, Josh."

False alarm, Josh thought as he drifted off to sleep again.

"Zip the tent! Zip the tent!" he heard someone calling. Quickly sitting up, Josh looked around. Brittany and Ella were already scrambling for the tent opening.

"Where's Mom?" Josh asked.

"I think she went to the van to get something," Brittany explained.

"What's going on?" Will called sleepily.

"Mom left to go to the van, but she called back to zip the tent," Ella filled him in.

"I think I know why. Look," Josh said.

Brittany, Will, and Ella looked out the tent windows too and saw a bear sauntering down the road.

"Whew, it passed our campsite," Brittany whispered.

The next campsite was not so fortunate. "You, bear, get out of here!" a man's voice called. They heard clapping and a woman's voice saying, "Go away!"

Above them at another campsite, the Reeds could see a ranger scanning the woods with his flashlight.

Suddenly, the Reeds heard a shuffling noise coming toward their tent. A large paw swiped the tent, and Josh saw claw marks appear in the tent fabric.

The kids were frozen in fear. In the same instant headlights shone on the bear, and Mom honked the horn.

The bear lumbered away. Mom rushed to the tent. "Is everyone okay?"

Everyone felt a little shaken but fine. Amazingly, Isaac and Dad had slept through it all. Although it was difficult for the others to get back to sleep after the bear encounter, they eventually did. It was calm the rest of the night.

The next morning, Will woke everyone with the announcement, "Let's go swimming!"

A nearby river did look inviting–not too fast and not too big. Dad and the kids decided to swim while Mom, acting as lifeguard, watched from the shore. Ella stayed with Isaac in the water since he was not a strong swimmer yet.

Josh thought the river bottom felt interesting. He walked on a combination of stone, sand, and mud.

"Look at these tiny clams," Dad called. "We can collect these to cook and eat later." Brittany, Will, and Josh began to hunt for clams too.

Then they heard, "Help, Dad!"

"Dan, over there!" Mom called and pointed.

Josh looked toward Ella and Isaac. They had wandered into an area of the river with a faster flow. Ella was holding Isaac, but the current was pulling them downstream. Dad was heading toward them as Ella found a crack in the rocks and held on.

When Dad reached them, he pulled them into the slower current again. Dad held onto Isaac while Ella pulled herself up onto a grayish white rock to rest. "Thanks, Dad."

The Reeds continued traveling through the Central Valley, which gradually ended in rolling hills. Josh saw moist areas in the coastal range.

Suddenly, thick forests surrounded them, and they saw what they were searching for–the redwoods. The massive trees' needles, tiny cones, and smell reminded Josh of Douglas-fir Christmas trees, only much bigger.

They decided to stop at Henry Cowell Redwoods State Park. Standing at the bottom and looking up was impressive, but they were not as massive as the sequoias.

"Where are we going next?" Josh asked.

Dad pulled out Nana's clues and read clue number fifteen:

> From sea to shining sea,
> That is where you'll be.
> You started near the Atlantic
> And traveled to the ____________.

Brittany spoke up. "I remember this one from studying oceans. We are almost to the Pacific."

"Let's go then!" Josh said and then added, "Since we have gone all the way across the country, shouldn't we be finding Nana soon?"

Dad looked at the clues. "I think so. There are only two clues left."

That would end the treasure hunt, Josh thought, but would he ever be able to solve the mystery?

The Reeds were not far from the Pacific Ocean. As they drove, it seemed strange to Josh to see evergreens growing in the same area as palm trees although he did not see them growing right next to each other. Soon through the fog they saw water in the distance. A cheer erupted: "The Pacific Ocean!" They had made it across America.

The next day the Reeds went to the beach at Natural Bridges State Park. Josh was exploring the tide pools with his family. "Ow! Got him!" Josh held up a crab. Dad found something too. He was touching sea anemones, which made them curl up.

Crash! The waves hit the rocks and splashed up into the tide pools, getting the Reeds wet.

"Since we're already soaked, let's go for a swim," Will called. The other kids joined him in the cold Pacific Ocean.

Josh went out into the waist-deep water and saw a wave behind him. Then he walked forward until the white-capped wave was almost ready to break on him. He caught the wave and body surfed into shore. "That was great!" he yelled. Soon all of them were body surfing.

The next wave Josh did not catch quite right. It tumbled him over and over under the water. Even though he came up choking on saltwater, he was ready to try it again.

After this, the Reeds rode cable cars in San Francisco and walked over the Golden Gate Bridge.

The next day, the boys wanted to swim one last time in the Pacific Ocean.

Josh was swimming in the water when he sensed something behind him. He turned just as a large object reached him. *Shark!* he thought. No, it was a big friendly dog bounding toward him. Will doubled over with laughter at the look on Josh's face.

A short time later, though, a dark round object appeared in the waves. "What's that?" Josh pointed.

"I don't know, but I'm not going to stay in the water and find out," Will decided as he stepped with quick high steps to get to the shore.

"That's a sea lion," a park official called.

After surviving their swim with dogs and sea lions, the guys showered and dressed while Brittany and Ella looked for sand dollars.

Back in the van, Dad read Nana's second to last clue:

Watch out for moose, buffalo, and bear
Watch out for geysers shooting into the air!

Will knew right away. "Where else would it be? Yellowstone is the place to be!"He grinned. "I'm getting into this rhyming thing. Maybe sometime I'll write some clues."

Chapter 19

Yellow Stones and Yellowstone

"Anyone want to pan for gold?" Dad called to the back seats of the van.

The Reed kids looked up from the cards they were secretly making for Mom's birthday. "Sure," Josh said.

"That sounds fun," Brittany joined in, and the others agreed.

"Sutter's Mill, here we come!" Dad said. He paused. "Hmm. I wonder how many people have said that."

Soon they arrived in Coloma, California, at the site of a major gold strike in 1848. Long ago when people heard that gold had been found at Sutter's Mill, they had come pouring in, hoping to strike it rich too.

"Look, it's Sutter's Mill, or at least a replica of the sawmill," Dad said.

As the Reeds walked around, Josh had an idea. "Let's imagine we're miners that have come looking for gold."

Will saw a miner's cabin and played along. "Come on over to my cabin and make yourself comfortable." He looked in the cabin. "Well, it sure doesn't look too comfortable, but it's better than the old jail."

Sure enough. The remains of the old jail could still be seen.

Brittany decided to join the game. "Well, I'm going to visit the stable and pick out a suitable buggy."

Josh led them over to the mining equipment. "And I'll get a look at this gear."

The Reeds visited the museum and then spent the rest of their time in the cold American River panning for gold. "I found some gold flakes!" Brittany called.

"Me too!" Isaac yelled.

Dad took a look. "They do look golden yellow, but it's probably mica or fool's gold rather than real gold."

"Gold or not, this is a good place to be on such a hot day," Ella said. The cold water flowing briskly through the rocks did feel good.

That evening the Reeds found a nice camping spot next to a cold stream in the cool Sierra Nevada Mountains where they could celebrate Mom's birthday.

After a dinner of fried chicken they had bought, the kids gave Mom the cards they had made. Dad gave her a road-runner figure as a trip memento. Ella and Brittany had wanted to buy a cake but couldn't find one. Instead, they stuck candles in a lemon twist pastry. After they sang "Happy Birthday," Ella asked, "I know it's not the party that we would have given you if we were home, but do you like it?"

Mom hugged Ella. "Of course I do. Being with my family and seeing the country with all of you is very special. Thank you for working to make this evening even more special. I feel very blessed indeed."

The next day the Reeds crossed into Nevada. They left the Sierra Nevada Mountains and drove into the Great Basin. Josh looked around at the flat land covered with sagebrush and surrounded by mountains. It did look like a giant bowl to him. Brittany was hoping to see a wild mustang but did not see any of the wild horses.

In Oregon they entered a different time zone. They changed from Pacific time to Mountain time and reset their watches.

When they entered Idaho, they were ready to find a place to camp. *What a lot of traveling today,* Josh thought. He hoped they would get to Yellowstone soon.

The next day Will said, "I feel like eating potato chips." Josh looked out the window and saw fields of Idaho's famous potatoes. He also saw fields of corn, barley, and hay.

Then Josh noticed a sign. "Look, it says, 'Prevent Range Fires.'"

"And there's a range fire!" Will said.

Almost immediately after seeing the sign, black smoky fields appeared. Then they saw red flames and people working to put the fire out.

The following day, the Reeds were finally close to Yellowstone. "Slow down!" Mom cried out. A coyote crossed the road in front of them.

"Cool!" Will exclaimed. "I hope we see lots of animals."

"Let's find a campsite first where we can leave the Explorer while we visit Yellowstone." A nearby state park was a good spot to leave their box trailer and look around.

"There are so many beautiful flowers here," Brittany enthused.

"Yes," Mom agreed, "and the lodgepole pines are lovely too."

"Let's go see those geysers!" Josh said excitedly.

The Reeds piled in the van, drove out of Idaho, through a tiny bit of Montana, and into Wyoming. *Surely by now we have lost whoever was following us,* Josh thought.

As they drove into Yellowstone National Park, they noticed stopped vehicles with people inside.

"Why are those cars parked beside the road?" Josh asked.

"There's an animal out there!" Isaac said excitedly.

Dad pulled over too, and the Reeds jumped out with cameras in hand.

"I see it," Dad said. "It's a bull elk."

"Look at the antlers on that thing," Will commented.

"How can it even walk between the trees without getting those antlers stuck?" Brittany wondered.

Slowly and quietly, the Reed kids snuck up on the animal. They were able to take some close-up pictures before the elk walked away.

The Reeds returned to the van but soon stopped again when they saw more cars beside the road. "Oh, how adorable!" Brittany exclaimed. A group of mother and baby elk grazed and rested nearby.

A short time later the Reeds were out walking on the paths when Isaac smelled something. "What's so stinky?" Isaac said as he held his nose.

"Something sure smells," Josh agreed.

"Like rotten eggs," Brittany decided.

"Actually, it's sulfur dioxide," Dad explained. "We're getting close to Yellowstone's famous mud pots, hot springs, and geysers."

"Remember to stay on the path," Mom instructed.

Soon the Reeds saw mud bubbling and hot noisy water bubbling and steaming.

"Why is it doing that?" Isaac asked.

"When water drips down to the hot lava below, it heats up. The water then boils up to the surface," Dad told him.

The Reeds then joined thousands of people waiting in a half circle around a white steaming hill. "Let's see," Mom said, looking at her watch. "Old Faithful erupts every thirty-five minutes to two hours, but the park ranger thinks it should be soon."

It was not long before steam and water shot 150 feet into the air. "Amazing!" Dad exclaimed.

Ella was quietly thinking. "Isn't it amazing too that all of these people are here to see the faithfulness of a geyser? I think people want to see something that they can count on not to change. I just wish everyone knew the One who is faithfully there for us. He never changes."

"You mean God?" Josh said.

"Yes," Ella said.

Mom smiled. "Maybe if we are faithful in our own lives to love each other and pray for others, it will help others to know the One who is the most faithful."

"Oh, don't step there!" Will suddenly broke in. Josh had been walking backwards as he tried to get a good picture of Old Faithful.

Too late. "Eww!" Brittany said as Josh put one foot in a pile of buffalo manure.

Thankfully, it had dried and did not stick to his shoe too much.

"Buffalo chips!" Will exclaimed. "Hey, the good news is that buffalo must be around," he said hopefully as he scanned the area.

"Oh, Josh, is that the man you saw following us?" Will asked as he pointed to a person in the distance.

Josh could not tell for sure. He was too far away. "Let me see your binoculars," Josh said.

As he focused the binoculars, the man quickly ran for the cover of some trees. "I couldn't tell," Josh said, "but it was suspicious that he ran away when he noticed us looking at him."

The Reeds returned to the van and drove until they saw cars quickly parked at strange angles. Then a large, hairy buffalo walked right in front of them, causing a buffalo traffic jam.

When they could drive some more, they soon saw hundreds of buffalo on a distant hill. "I hope they don't stampede," Will joked. That was just the beginning. Later, they saw more groups of buffalo on a nearby hill.

Josh and Brittany burst into song. "Oh, give me a home where the buffalo roam..." The others laughed but joined in too.

After watching some trumpeter swans and pelicans floating on the water, the Reeds returned to camp.

It was getting cold, with temperatures heading into the 40s that night. *Only one more clue to read,* Josh thought. Soon they would come to the end of the treasure hunt, but would the mystery be solved in time? For that matter, would it ever be solved?

Chapter 20

The Chase

"Let's hunt for moose with cameras," Josh said hopefully.

Will's eyes sparkled mischievously. "If you see some moose holding cameras, I really want to see that."

"That's not what I meant. I mean we have the cameras and find the moose," Josh said even though he knew Will already understood perfectly.

They hunted for moose near the water. "Is that a moose?" Isaac called.

They walked closer and Will looked through his binoculars. "No, just a fisherman up to his waist in the water," Will said.

After several more false alarms, the Reeds decided it was time to visit the Grand Canyon of the Yellowstone. The Yellowstone River dropped in a large waterfall into the canyon.

"Look at the colors," Brittany said, sighing. Yellow, orange, and red streaked the canyon walls while evergreen trees growing on every available ledge dotted the canyon with green.

"See any moose or bears?" Josh asked as he looked around. The Reeds scanned the forest.

"I'm looking, but nothing is jumping out at me," Will joked.

Even on this warm summer day, the Reeds could see patches of snow resting on the mountaintops in the distance. "Let's get a closer look at that snow," Dad said suddenly.

The Reeds drove toward the Grand Tetons, crossing the Continental Divide three times. "That sign says we are 8,391feet in the air, way above sea level," Dad said.

"That's the highest we've been!" Josh said excitedly.

"It sure beats Death Valley when we were 282 feet *below* sea level," Will remembered.

Ice and snow could easily be seen now. They stopped to take pictures and then continued on because Dad wanted to find a particular kind of spot. He found it at Jackson Lake.

Mom grabbed his hand. "This is the most beautiful place I have ever seen," she exclaimed.

"It looks like a painting," Ella agreed.

"Or a postcard," Brittany added.

The rugged snowy mountains touched the sky while their green, pine-covered lower sections rested near the blue lake. The mountains were reflected in the water, but the lake itself was clear with multicolored stones on the lake bottom.

"Let's go swimming!" Josh said enthusiastically.

Unfortunately, their swimsuits were packed in the Explorer, which they had not brought on this steep climb into the mountains. That did not stop the boys, who just splashed into the lake with their pants on. "Cold, cold, cold!" Josh yelled.

"But refreshing!" Will called back.

Brittany, Ella, and Mom rolled up their pant legs and waded into the cool water. "I feel like I'm in an aquarium," Brittany called to Josh.

Josh looked down. Around his toes, the little fish darted through the clear water over the colorful stones.

Returning to Yellowstone, the Reeds dried off and then resumed moose hunting. "I see an elk," Brittany said.

"And I see some mule deer." Mom pointed them out to the others.

"I see a buffalo," Isaac said.

"Me too!" Brittany and Josh said together and laughed. This buffalo was hard to miss. It stood four feet from the side of their car now.

"Can I pet it?" Isaac asked.

"I don't think that would be a good idea. It's a wild animal," Mom explained. "But you can take its picture."

"I think that buffalo must work for a camera company," Dad joked as they snapped pictures left and right.

Driving on, the Reeds saw cars parked at crazy angles on the road. "Look! Look!" Brittany pointed. "It's a mother and baby moose!"

The Reeds quickly parked and climbed out of the van to get a better view. In a grassy area in the forest below, the mother and baby moose quietly grazed. The kids went a little closer to take pictures but not too close. They certainly did not want to make that large mother moose feel like she needed to protect her baby.

Josh had a thought. "Do you know that we have not seen even one bear at Yellowstone, even though people always talk about the bears at Yellowstone?"

"That's okay," Brittany answered her twin. "Other people can have a turn to see the bears. We have seen enough on this trip already."

That night the Reeds camped in Shoshone National Forest. This was still bear territory. As Josh drifted off to sleep, he wondered if they would have any night visitors.

Josh suddenly sat up, wide awake. He wondered what it was that had awakened him. A light flashed. A twig broke. *That's no bear,* Josh thought. Carefully, quietly, he lifted the flap and looked out into the dark night. By the light of the moon, Josh saw the form of a man holding a camera. *Of course,* Josh thought. The flashes of light were from a camera taking pictures of them!

Josh crawled to where his dad lay sleeping and shook him awake. Josh handed him a flashlight and pointed to the tent door. "The intruder is here," Josh barely whispered.

His dad snuck to the tent door, very quietly put on his shoes, and unzipped the flap.

As his dad exited the tent, the movement alerted the stranger outside. He turned and raced into the woods.

Dan Reed did not want to let him get away to continue shadowing his family. Dan raced after the man and his bobbing flashlight. Even though the moon gave some light, Dan had to turn on his own flashlight so he would not stumble and fall on the shadowy, uneven ground.

Suddenly, the stranger's flashlight went out. Headlights appeared, and the stranger roared away in his car. Discouraged, Dan Reed returned to camp.

Josh had awakened the others. They were waiting in the tent. "Did you see him?" Josh asked.

"I did," his dad answered, "but I couldn't catch him. He got away in his car."

"I wonder what he wants," Brittany said with concern.

"I don't know, but let's not get too worried. After all, he actually helped Josh when he was lost," Dad reminded them. "I would like to talk to him, though. What we need is a way to catch him."

"I've got just the thing, Dad," Will said with a great big smile.

Chapter 21

The Treasure

Will told the others his plan.

"That just might work," Dad said with approval.

Whoever that man was, the Reeds figured that Dad had scared him off for the night, so after plans had been made for the following night, the Reeds went back to sleep.

In the morning, it was time to read Nana's final clue. "I almost don't want this adventure to end," Josh admitted.

"But soon we will get to see Nana," Brittany reminded him.

"And there is a treasure involved," Will added. "Since Josh is our own family detective, I think he should solve the last clue." The others agreed.

"Thanks, everyone," Josh said as Dad handed him the clue. He read:

> Don't rush past this mountain of faces;
> Look some more. I'll be there.

Josh looked at the clue. "Rush and more are underlined. If we put the words together, it says 'Rushmore.'" Josh thought about famous places he had read about. "I know! A mountain with the faces of important presidents carved into it is Mt. Rushmore!"

It was their last destination on the treasure hunt. The Reeds packed up and started out.

Josh saw a river cutting through the towering mountains but wondered how they would get through those mountains. At first the Reeds drove through a pass, but then it looked like the road would end right there in front of a huge mountain. "Uh, Dad, where does the road go?" Josh asked.

"I don't know," Dad answered cheerfully. "The unknown–that's what makes it an adventure."

The road did come to the mountain and then continued right through it. They entered a long dark tunnel cut through the granite and drove through to the other side.

The road took them higher and higher into the Big Horn Mountains. It was then that the van started having problems. It jolted several times and died at Powder River Pass at an elevation of 9,666 feet above sea level.

Dad figured it was the vapor lock having a problem. While Dad looked through the van owner's manual, the others stepped outside to stretch their legs. Evergreen trees and grass still grew way up there.

"I'll race you!" Will told Josh.

"Wait up!" Brittany called.

Soon Will, Josh, Isaac, and Brittany were ready. They counted, "One, two, three, go!" and raced up a hill in the thin air. It was hard to catch their breath at this high elevation. They dropped to the ground to rest and looked at the rugged mountains and the sheep grazing in a grassy knoll just below them.

By the time Dad finished reading the owner's manual, the van started up again. Dad joked to Mom, "I guess if you ever have a problem with the vapor lock, just read the owner's manual and by the time you finish, the van will start again."

The family continued on their way. When they arrived at their campsite that night, they knew it was time to put their plan into operation.

First they set up camp like they normally did. "Now it's time for the secret weapon," Will stated with a phony accent.

He pulled out the motion detector alarm system he had made. "If it worked for Dad's car on our driveway, it should work here. It can detect motion for twenty-five feet anywhere in front of our tent. It should tell us if anyone is coming."

"Will it play loud music again?" Josh asked.

"No," Will assured him. "I made a few modifications." He grinned.

"Why did you even bring it on this trip?" Josh asked.

"I thought it might liven things up if our trip got boring. Besides, you never know when you might need a motion detector alarm system. It can come in handy."

"I guess so," Josh admitted.

That night the Reeds slept, ready with their shoes still on their feet. The tent door was only partially zipped. The motion detector was in place.

Then it happened. The family in the tent was awakened to the sound of Will's voice booming on the tape player, "Stop! Don't move! We have you surrounded! Put your hands up! We mean it! Put your hands up!"

Dad rushed out of the tent and tackled the stunned man, pinning him to the ground. "Boys, get me the rope!"

Josh and Will brought the rope and a flashlight. Dad tied him up while the man pleaded, "Wait, I can explain! I meant no harm. Please, you have to believe me."

The others came rushing out. "You got him!" Brittany said with relief.

Dad took the flashlight and shone it on the young man. Josh thought he looked to be about nineteen, not much older than Ella. "Okay, explain before I call the police. Who are you and why have you been following my family?" Dad demanded.

"My, my name is Chaz Lincoln," the young man stuttered. His words came out all jumbled. "I'm just a broke college student. This was supposed to be my summer job. She hired me. She wanted me to follow you and see where you were. I e-mailed her pictures of you."

"*Who* hired you?" Dad asked, running out of patience.

"Andrea Reed," the young man replied. "Your Nana."

Dad sat back. Everyone looked stunned. "Nana hired you?" As Dad let this information sink in, he began to think aloud. "She wanted to see where we were and keep track of our progress." Finally, a slow smile spread across his face. "Of course she did. Nana would."

A thought occurred to Josh. "How else would she know when to meet us at Mt. Rushmore? This guy would tell her when we would arrive."

"That's right, Mr. Reed," Chaz quickly affirmed.

"I think it's time to call Nana," Dad said as he pulled a cell phone out of his pocket. While the others waited, Dad called Nana's cell phone number.

"Hi, it's Dan." A pause. "It's good to hear your voice too. We have a certain Chaz Lincoln here with us."

After Dad finished the phone call, he turned to the others. "Nana did indeed hire him although we were never supposed to see him. She did not count on Josh's keen detective skills or Will's motion detector alarm system. Nana vouches for this young man's integrity. I think it's safe to untie him."

"Thank you, sir. Thank you," said Chaz as they untied his ropes.

The Reeds slept until morning. Then the Reeds in their van, followed by Chaz wearing sunglasses in his sleek black car, drove to Mt. Rushmore in South Dakota.

Josh felt elated. The mystery was solved. He had been right after all. In his detective journal, he could finally write how the light flashes, black car, and man taking their picture were all connected. Of course, without Will's motion detector and Dad's tackling skills, they might never have caught him and discovered the truth. It was more than just his own observing and thinking, Josh knew.

Arriving at Mt. Rushmore, the Reeds left the van and walked to a good viewing spot. "Look at those stone heads," Isaac said.

"They do have stony expressions," Will tried to say with a straight face.

"Let's see," Josh thought as he stared at the huge faces carved into the mountain. "That must be George Washington, the first president, and Abraham Lincoln, and Thomas Jefferson." He stopped.

"Don't forget Theodore Roosevelt," Brittany chimed in.

"Thanks, Brittany," Josh said.

"I see Nana's face," Isaac said.

"No, these are the faces of presidents," Josh tried to explain.

Isaac jumped up and down. "Not there. Nana's face is over there!" Isaac pointed toward the crowd of people coming their way.

"Nana!" Brittany called with delight. Nana rushed to them and tried to hug them all at once.

Her words came out in a rush. "My dears, I am so glad you are here! Did you have a grand adventure? It was so much fun to see pictures of you and where you were. I am terribly sorry that Chaz frightened you. Now, let's go find a quiet place to visit."

They found a grassy place to sit down. "This time *you* are the ones with amazing tales of an adventure," Nana said happily. "Tell me all!"

The Reeds took turns telling Nana about the bear, tornado, storm, cliff-climbing, rattlesnake, Josh getting lost in a cave and in the sequoias, and more. "It was the best treasure hunt in the world!" Josh added.

Nana listened thoughtfully and smiled. "I think you have found a treasure far better than what I have for you. In your travels, I can tell you have recognized the treasure of each other. When you can see how special are the people who love you and whom you love, you have found a treasure indeed. You helped each other and enjoyed doing things together. Of course, the greatest treasure of all is knowing God and being a part of *His* family."

"You are a treasure too," Brittany said as she got up and gave Nana another hug. "Thanks for planning this treasure hunt for us."

"Yes, thank you," the others echoed.

"Now, now. You found me, yes, but I still need to give you the treasure I promised."

Nana pulled a large wooden jewelry box out of her bag and handed it to Mom. The others gathered around to see. When Mom opened the ornately carved box, the first thing they saw were coins.

"First of all," Nana said. "There are state quarters for each of you from every state through which you traveled. They will remind you of the places you have been."

"Thank you, Nana."

"Now look on the bottom," Nana continued.

Mom dug to the bottom of the box and found seven tickets. "There is one for each of you," Nana explained. "Now that you have had a taste of adventure, I'm sure you will want more. I want to send you to Alaska!"

"Alaska?" Mom was stunned.

Nana smiled. "I know you need time to recover from this adventure first, but when you are ready, the tickets are yours. Don't worry. It is not a camping trip this time. This, my dears, is an all-expense-paid vacation on a luxury cruise ship."

The Reeds cheered. "Camping was actually fun," Brittany said, "but a cruise ship sounds wonderful!"

Josh smiled and thought to himself, *I'll be glad to go on an Alaskan adventure, especially if I can find another mystery to solve.*

Printed in the United States
206609BV00001B/196-246/P

9 781606 476383